THE FAITH IN FLOWERS

a Poppy Creek novel

RACHAEL BLOOME

Cover Design: Ana Grigoriu-Voicu with Books-Design.

Editing: Beth Attwood

Proofing: Krista Dapkey with KD Proofreading

SERIES READING ORDER

The Clause in Christmas

The Truth in Tiramisu

The Secret in Sandcastles

The Meaning in Mistletoe

The Faith in Flowers

The Whisper in Wind

For anyone in need of a new beginning....

2 Corinthians 5:17

LETTER FROM THE AUTHOR

ear friend,
    A small piece of my heart goes into each book I write, and although it's completely fictional, this is my most personal story yet. I'm so grateful I could explore the themes in this novel from a place of peace and thankfulness.

If you're still searching for hope and healing, or have questions after reading this book, I'd love to share more about the gift of grace I've received and how it changed my life. You can reach me at hello@rachaelbloome.com.

And if you'd like to learn more about my own redemption story, you can read my blogpost, An Unlikely Author, which I've included at the end.

But first, I hope you enjoy your visit back to Poppy Creek to reconnect with old friends and meet new ones, too.

BLESSINGS & BLOOMS,
Rachael Bloome

*P*ale and petrified, Olivia Parker dug her manicured nails into the armrest of seat 27C.

She hated flying under the best of circumstances, but being tossed around in turbulence somewhere over the Midwest topped her list of unpleasant experiences.

Plus, the sleeping pill she'd taken had only made her loopy.

Not to mention, uncharacteristically loose-lipped.

"You were saying, dearie?" The little old lady sitting in 27B paused her plastic knitting needles to pat Olivia's hand.

How she managed to remain calm enough to knit, Olivia would never know. Any moment now, she feared the thin, tapered objects would become lodged somewhere unfortunate.

"I-I was?" she stammered, reaching for the half-empty water bottle jammed into the seat back in front of her.

The plastic crinkled as she yanked it from its resting place, and a young mother across the aisle flinched.

Olivia offered an apologetic smile as she unscrewed the cap.

Clearly, she wasn't the only one on edge.

"You were saying how you're not going to tell your family

about your divorce," the woman reminded her, resuming her knitting.

Even as Olivia chugged the cool water, her throat remained uncomfortably dry and constricted.

Oh, how she wished she could go back in time and redo the last twenty minutes.

She would have kept her mouth shut.

How could she explain the complicated dynamics of her family to a complete stranger? How her mother—and everyone else in her hometown—had put her on a pedestal. Or how she'd left her disaster of a life in New York City to help plan her brother's wedding in Poppy Creek. She couldn't show up on his doorstep and blurt out, *My husband left me and true love is a soul-crushing lie. Oh, and by the way, would you prefer a band or a DJ at the reception?*

Without responding, Olivia stuffed the water bottle back inside the seat pocket.

"Is that why you're still wearing your ring?" the woman asked, apparently content to carry on the conversation without Olivia's participation. With a bob of her white curls, she nodded toward Olivia's left hand, which had reclaimed its tense grip on the armrest.

Olivia's gaze fell to the object in question.

The flawless two-carat diamond in a chic platinum setting stared back at her with a pitying glint. After Steven's betrayal, she should have chucked it into the Hudson River. Or into one of the many piles of horse manure perfuming Central Park.

But she couldn't bring herself to take it off. She'd slid it all the way up to her knuckle once. But that's as far as she could go.

Pathetic, considering Steven abandoned her almost ten months ago.

Not to mention what happened on Christmas morning....

She involuntarily shuddered at the thought.

"Cold, dear?"

Olivia met the woman's kind eyes. She suspected that if she said yes, the grandmotherly stranger would give her the afghan-in-progress.

"I'm fine. Thank you."

Okay, so she was far from fine. But not because of the frigid air that smelled faintly of stale coffee and collective fear.

She'd given her heart to Steven, vowing *'til death do us part.* Divorce had never—and wouldn't have ever—crossed her mind. How had he tossed her aside so easily?

Scrunching her eyes shut, she battled the unwanted memories of the evening that had catapulted her into oblivion.

They'd just concluded the most perfect meal at their favorite restaurant. The warm night air had wafted through the open windows of the town car as they sat side by side in the back seat. Not close enough that their thighs touched, but not on opposite ends, either. Nothing to indicate the life-altering devastation that loomed ahead.

They'd even discussed asking the driver to drop them off a block from their apartment so they could walk the rest of the way home and savor the remainder of the pleasant evening.

Then, as casually as if reporting the next day's weather forecast, Steven announced that he no longer loved her.

No tears. No tremor in his voice. Not even a twinge of remorse.

As Olivia sat in stunned silence, Steven had the driver stop in front of their building. She'd never forget his condescending expression as he opened the car door and warned her not to make a scene. As if, heaven forbid, she might embarrass him.

He'd left her standing alone on the sidewalk completely shell-shocked.

For months, she couldn't figure out what had happened. She'd begged him to reconsider, promising to change, to do whatever he wanted to make things work between them.

It wasn't until Christmas morning that—

A sharp cry tore Olivia from her thoughts.

As the plane shook, the young mother tried to soothe her terrified toddler, her cheeks red with embarrassment.

"The poor dear," the older woman cooed, her wrinkled brow furrowed with concern.

Impulsively, Olivia tugged her carry-on from beneath the seat. She unzipped the main compartment and withdrew the toy she'd brought for her nephew, Ben. She could always buy a new one when they landed in San Francisco.

If they landed, that is.

She passed the trendy action figure to the harried mother, who politely refused.

But when Olivia insisted, and the toddler's eyes lit up with delight, she gratefully accepted.

"That was very thoughtful." Her neighbor smiled, regarding her with warmth.

Olivia shifted in her seat, uncomfortable with the open admiration. She certainly didn't deserve it. "I just hope it helps. And that we arrive safely at SFO."

"We will."

"How can you be so sure?" Olivia hoped her composed companion had some unexpected aeronautical expertise as well as unflappable knitting skills.

"You just have to have a little faith, my dear."

Olivia barely suppressed a snort.

Faith? Was she kidding?

She'd had faith in her husband's unconditional love. And look where that had gotten her.

Faith was a fantasy she couldn't afford.

She was in full-on survival mode.

First, she needed to make it back on solid ground.

Then, she had to get through the next few weeks without ruining her brother's wedding with the depressing news of her divorce.

Luckily, she had plenty of practice keeping secrets.

*W*ith his arms crossed and eyes closed, Reed Hollis leaned against the side of his vintage VW van, relishing the warmth of the late afternoon sun on his upturned face. The pleasant aroma of sugary kettle corn mingled with the sweet, floral scent of lavender and tea roses, and he took a deep breath, filling his lungs with the enticing mix.

Every year, he looked forward to Poppy Creek's farmers market season. He enjoyed the hustle and bustle of locals and tourists meandering in the town square buying fresh produce and artisan goods like specialty pastries and hand-dipped caramel apples. The live music and art demonstrations made the evenings feel like a can't-miss event.

Plus, they were great for business. Most nights, he packed up his van—which he'd renovated into a kitschy flower-shop-and-delivery vehicle—without a single stem left. The busy spring and summer months more than compensated for the winter lull.

All in all, the modest operation landed him a decent living.

Of course, he never imagined his life would turn out this way. By thirty, he'd expected to have a big, boisterous family and a thriving farm to call his own. Instead, he ran a small nursery and remained a confirmed bachelor. The last of his friend group to settle down, he planned on staying single indefinitely.

He'd risked love once and his heart had been crushed like a clump of dried rose petals.

But still, he could hardly complain. He loved his hometown and his close-knit community. Although his parents divorced a few years ago and his younger brother had moved away, he still shared a five-acre parcel of land with his mother and he frequently walked to her cottage for home-cooked meals.

Not a bad life, all things considered.

"Where are the snapdragons?" The note of disappointment in the woman's tone yanked Reed from his contented state.

As his eyelids fluttered open, he immediately stiffened.

Harriet Parker gazed at his dwindling selection of bouquets with a pinched expression.

Ever since the Parkers moved into town his freshman year of high school, Reed found the woman intimidating. A former New York City socialite, she'd made it clear from day one that he wasn't good enough to associate with her children. Which made life complicated considering they lived on the other side of the creek from each other and her son, Grant, was his own age.

But despite Harriet's disapproval, he and Grant became good friends. And to add to her consternation, Reed befriended Grant's younger sister, Olivia, as well. His heart had gone out to the shy and awkward girl. She'd avoided the rest of the kids in town with dogged resolve and spent most of her time at the creek dividing their properties. But even with their three-year age gap, they had a lot in common.

At least, they *used* to....

"I didn't bring any snapdragons today," Reed told her, conjuring his best customer-service voice. "But I have some nice gladiolus you might like."

The crease in her brow deepened. "I was really hoping for snapdragons. They're Olivia's favorite."

Reed's heartbeat stuttered. Olivia? He knew she'd be coming home for Grant's wedding, but it was still weeks away.

"Any chance you can bring some by the house later? I'll pay extra for delivery, of course." She smiled, and to Reed's surprise, the warmth reached all the way to her usually cold and piercing eyes.

During the previous year—ever since some awful secrets from Harriet's past came to light—she'd been trying to turn over a new leaf and make amends. And while her efforts seemed genuine, Reed still found the shift in her demeanor jarring.

"Sure. Do you prefer any particular time?"

"Before five thirty, if possible. Olivia should be home around six, and I'd like to have everything ready before she arrives. She visits so rarely. I'd like to make things perfect for her while she's in town helping Grant and Eliza with the wedding."

Right. He should have guessed. As an event planner for New York's finest, it only made sense she'd lend her skills to help her brother. Especially since Grant's fiancée, Eliza, seemed determined to make their wedding the most spectacular event Poppy Creek had ever seen.

"Five thirty won't be a problem. In fact, I can probably make it even earlier." He suspected he'd sell out in another hour or so. And if he were honest, he wanted a generous buffer between his delivery and Olivia's arrival.

"Perfect. Thank you, Reed." She reached into her wallet and slid out several crisp bills, tipping him way more than necessary. "Now, I'm off to The Calendar Café. Eliza made one of her tiramisu cheesecakes for dessert tonight, and I can't wait for Olivia to try it. I've been telling her it's better than any cheesecake she'd find in New York."

"That's high praise. And I'd have to agree." He found himself returning her smile.

If someone had told him a few years ago that he'd exchange pleasantries with Harriet Parker, he wouldn't have believed it.

Although, he knew from experience that people could change —for better or for worse.

Usually, it was the latter.

At least, that had been the case with his father.

And Olivia. He missed the kindhearted country girl with bare feet and dirt under her fingernails.

He still felt a stab of humiliation whenever he thought about the phone call he'd made over the holidays.

Of course, she'd never called him back.

Since the moment she got engaged, their friendship had withered on the vine. And maybe it was a good thing it had. He couldn't exactly picture them having long chats about her amazing married life to Steven Rockford III. Not without wanting to rip his heart out of his chest with gardening shears.

No, they were better off keeping their distance.

Which is exactly what he intended to do for the next few weeks.

CHAPTER TWO

*A*s her rental car zipped around another curve in the winding mountain road, Olivia clutched the steering wheel with all her might, trying to recall the last time she'd driven a car.

Although Steven owned a classic Porsche, he preferred to be chauffeured. While she found the practice a little pretentious, it also made getting around the city a million times easier, so she'd become accustomed to it.

Which had become the pattern with most things in her life—Steven's preferences had slowly taken over their day-to-day habits until they became the status quo. Now that she had to think for herself, she wasn't sure what she wanted anymore.

Did she enjoy having a driver and dining out at restaurants every night? And what about the morning treks to the upscale coffee shop after their hour-long gym sessions?

Once, she'd suggested brewing their own coffee at home so they could leisurely sip a cup or two in bed. Steven had stared at her as though she'd proposed wearing khaki capris to the Met Gala. Although, to be fair, their matching duvet and sheets were white Egyptian cotton. Not exactly stain friendly.

Shame crept up her neck, blazing across her cheeks as she thought about everything she'd given up in the divorce. She'd been so naive, believing if she didn't make a fuss, he'd realize he was on the brink of a huge mistake and take her back. Which meant agreeing to give him everything except for her event-planning business and their swanky apartment that she could barely afford on her own.

She shook away the painful memory as her eyes welled with tears, blurring the bridge up ahead. Blinking rapidly, she tried to focus.

Almost home....

Even after the nightmare flight and purchasing a new toy for Ben in San Francisco, she'd made better time than she'd expected. And all she wanted was to say a quick hello to her parents and slip upstairs for a relaxing shower before an early bedtime. She'd been so grateful when Grant and Eliza said they wouldn't come over until tomorrow, giving her time to rest and recharge after her tiring flight.

After a handful of video calls, she couldn't wait to meet her nephew in person, but she'd be much better company after a decent night's sleep. Considering she'd avoided most social interactions since her divorce, she was a little rusty.

As she turned down her parents' peaceful lane, she almost felt the hot shower easing the tension in her muscles, rinsing away layers of airport germs and even more layers of repressed emotions.

Fortunately, no one would be able to hear her quiet sobs over the sound of rushing water.

An elegant Cape Cod-style home came into view, flooding Olivia with bittersweet memories. Her father had uprooted their lives in New York, moving the family to the quaint town of Poppy Creek when she was eleven years old. Although he'd never said a word to defend his decision—even amid her mother's vehement protests—Olivia knew why. And she'd never loved her father more.

She parked behind a vintage VW van, her heart hammering when her gaze fell on the bold lettering painted on the side.

Reed's Roses.

What was Reed Hollis doing here?

For the briefest of seconds, she thought she might actually be happy to see him. But her excitement quickly turned to dread, then guilt.

After several years of silence, he'd reached out to her over the holidays and she'd sent him straight to voice mail. Although she'd had a good reason, she'd never called him back to explain.

He must think the worst of her—a realization that made her chest ache.

The dull throb intensified when he stepped out of the van.

Although he looked unassuming in faded jeans and a plain cotton tee, Olivia's throat went dry. His tall, tanned physique rippled with muscles he didn't have in high school. And he wore his dark, hickory-colored hair shorter now, which drew attention to his strong jawline and intense, soulful brown eyes.

Eyes she used to get lost in whenever he went on long tangents about soil acidity and complicated hybridization techniques. Even at fourteen, he'd already known what he wanted to do with his life—a trait she'd always admired.

It took her a moment to register the cluster of sherbet-colored snapdragons in his hand.

Was he greeting her with a bouquet of her favorite flowers?

She wasn't sure why her stomach somersaulted at the possibility.

They were friends, nothing more.

And truthfully, as much as it pained her to admit, they weren't even that anymore.

So, why exactly was he here?

*R*eed gripped the bouquet so tightly he feared the stems might snap.

Olivia Parker had been out of his life for years. Why did seeing her again feel like someone had punched him in the stomach?

It wasn't just her unnerving beauty. Although, she'd always been the most stunning woman he'd ever seen with her ink-black hair and eyes the color of lavender and bluebells combined.

No, the tingling sensation that reached all the way to his toes stemmed from far more than her outward appearance. And if he could stop the visceral reaction from happening, he would.

Olivia was a married woman. He couldn't go down the road of wishing things had turned out differently between them. She'd planted roots somewhere else—*with* someone else. He had no business harboring feelings for her. Of course, his brain knew that. But his heart stubbornly refused to listen.

Squaring his shoulders, he summoned a smile. "Welcome home."

A shadow of uncertainty clouded her features and her gaze fell to the flowers in his hand.

His pulse spiked as soon as he realized what she must be thinking. "These are for your mother."

Her eyes widened.

"I mean, for you. *From* your mother. Your mother ordered them for you," he corrected, fumbling over his words. What was wrong with him? They used to talk all the time. Even after she'd left for boarding school her sophomore year of high school, they'd kept in touch, spending several nights a week chatting on the phone about anything and everything. Now, he couldn't even form a single sentence without stammering.

Before she could respond, the front door flew open and Harriet Parker skipped down the steps toward them.

"You're early!" She flung her arms around her daughter, pulling her into an exuberant embrace.

Olivia met his gaze over her mother's shoulder and they exchanged a knowing glance.

Growing up, Harriet constantly impressed the importance of punctuality. And according to Harriet, showing up early was just as impolite as arriving late.

Olivia shot him a look that said, *Here comes another lecture.*

"It's wonderful!" Harriet cried, squeezing her tighter. "That means more time with my favorite daughter."

Reed suppressed a chuckle as Olivia gaped in surprise and mouthed, *What's happening?*

As he considered how many things had changed since Olivia's last visit—Grant learning he had a son, Harriet's personal transformation, and the positive shift in their family dynamic—he realized he wanted to be there for her as she processed it all. He missed being the person she confided in and counted on.

But someone else had that role now.

"Let's go inside, shall we?" Harriet pulled back with a broad smile, clearly ecstatic to have her daughter home. "Dinner won't be ready for a little while, but your brother and Eliza are on their way. They wanted to surprise you." As she ushered Olivia along the stone pathway, she paused as if noticing Reed for the first time. "Heavens! Have you been there the whole time?"

"Yes, ma'am. Just dropping these off." He held out the bouquet.

"Thank you, Reed. They're lovely." She gathered the bundle of vibrant peach and yellow blooms in her arm, adding, "Since you're here, you should join us for dinner."

Join them? He nearly choked on thin air. In all of the years he'd known the Parkers, he'd never once been invited over for dinner.

Olivia looked just as shocked at her mother's suggestion. And he couldn't tell if she liked the idea or hated it. His own thoughts on the subject were equally mixed.

"Thank you, but I really should be going. I don't want to impose on a family occasion."

"Nonsense." Harriet gave a dismissive wave. "The more the merrier. Besides, you were always such a good friend to Grant and Olivia. I should have invited you over years ago."

Although touched by her admission, Reed hesitated, debating the prudence of the invitation.

"Yes, please stay," Olivia added. "It is my welcome home dinner, after all. I'd love for you to join us."

His heart sank and soared at the same time. She wanted him to stay? How could he refuse now?

"Then I guess I don't have a choice," he said with a teasing grin.

She beamed in return and the sight of her smile sent a strange warmth rippling through him.

Yep. Dinner was definitely a bad idea.

CHAPTER THREE

*D*espite all the chatter at the dinner table and the excitement of finally meeting her nephew in person— whom she already adored even more than she believed possible— Olivia found her thoughts drifting to Reed.

She hadn't expected to ask him to stay. The words had escaped before she could stop them. But as irrational as it sounded, all the familiar emotions of their childhood friendship —the safety and comfort—had come rushing back in their brief exchange. He'd been her best friend once—a steady constant in her life. Until she'd had to cut ties for the sake of her marriage.

Maybe a silver lining in the wake of her divorce would be finding something she'd lost—the part of herself she'd abandoned when she left Poppy Creek.

If Reed could forgive her, that is.

There was just one niggling concern: something happened the moment she saw him standing there with the bouquet of her favorite flowers—a peculiar flutter in the pit of her stomach.

To distract herself, she turned to her eight-year-old nephew, Ben, who sat beside her. "How's school going?" She kept her gaze fixed on his sweet, heart-shaped face, ignoring the way Reed kept glancing in her direction from across the table.

"Okay, I guess. I don't like math, though." Ben jammed a spoonful of mashed potatoes into his mouth, and Olivia suppressed a laugh as he struggled to chew the generous helping.

"Me, neither. Which is why I use the calculator on my phone for everything."

"Don't give him any ideas," Grant warned her. "He's already asking for one."

"And we told him not until middle school, at least," Eliza added. "Kids spend way too much time on devices these days."

"You two didn't have that problem growing up." Harriet's eyes twinkled as she glanced between her children. "Grant, you and Eliza would practice your swing dancing every chance you got. And Olivia, you would leave the house after your homework and not come back until after dark. Usually covered in an inch of mud."

Olivia cast a sideways glance at Reed, who offered a sympathetic smile. They both knew how much her mother had hated the fact that she'd preferred playing outdoors—usually with Reed —to flipping through fashion magazines and hosting tea parties.

But Harriet merely chuckled, her soft gaze fixed on her husband, Stan, as though sharing a moment.

"Remember the time she rescued the injured possum?" he asked.

"How could I forget? I'd never seen anything so ugly in all my life."

"What you two didn't know," Grant interjected with a mischievous grin, "was that she kept it in our bathtub for two whole days before you found it."

"Tattletale!" Olivia made a face at her brother, who laughed it off.

"You had a pet possum?" Ben asked in amazement. "Can I have one?"

"No!" his parents cried in horrified unison.

The dining room erupted in laughter, and Olivia shared another smile with Reed across the table. She could get used to this new reality where all the people she cared about got along with each other. For most of her life, her family coexisted, but they weren't close, rarely spoke, and certainly never had this much fun together.

"These stories are priceless," Eliza said as her giggles subsided. "It's a shame Steven is missing them."

Olivia stiffened. So far, she'd managed to avoid the topic of her ex-husband. Since he traveled frequently as a figurehead for his family's investment company, it wasn't difficult to excuse his absence. Although, everyone expected him to arrive in time for the wedding, and she hadn't figured out how to handle that rather significant detail yet. For now, she needed to shift the topic of conversation in a different direction. "How are the wedding plans coming along?"

"Not great." Eliza exchanged a tentative glance with Grant before adding, "We had a bit of a setback."

Grant cleared his throat as he shifted in his seat.

"Whatever it is, I'm sure it's something we can fix." Olivia evoked her most assuring event-planner voice.

"It's the venue...." Eliza set down her fork with a dramatic sigh.

"Aren't you holding it at Sanders Farm?" Olivia had been pleased to hear they decided to have the wedding at the picturesque property. Mitch Sanders hosted nearly every major event in town, either in his rustic red barn or on the sprawling lawn. And since Eliza wanted the largest, grandest wedding in Poppy Creek history, there wasn't any other place suitable.

"That was the plan." Eliza's petite shoulders slumped, and Grant placed a hand over his fiancée's for moral support. "But Mitch is selling the farm, and he already has an interested party."

Trying to hide her concern, Olivia said calmly, "I never thought Mitch would sell. What happened?"

"It came as a shock to us, too," Grant confessed. "He inherited a fishing boat in Maine when his uncle passed away. Since he has family back East, he decided to embrace the opportunity for a fresh start."

"What's going to happen to the farm?" For as long as Olivia could remember, it had been a town institution.

Stan dabbed his mouth with a cloth napkin before returning it to his lap. "The rumor is that the new owners want a private weekend getaway from their stressful jobs in the city."

Silence filled the dining room, except for Ben's spoon scraping across his plate as he dug into his mashed potatoes, oblivious to the grown-up problems.

"How sad," Olivia murmured. The loss would be devastating to the town. "Where will people buy their Christmas trees? And what about the Daisy Hop and Christmas Eve dance?"

"No one knows." Stan gave a helpless shrug. "It will be a huge adjustment, that's for sure."

"So, we're basically back to square one," Eliza told her, bringing the conversation full circle. "The town square isn't big enough. We need triple the outdoor space and a kitchen for the caterers."

"And the wedding is only a few weeks away," Grant added glumly. "It seems impossible."

"Challenging, yes. But not impossible." Olivia dug deep to project the necessary confidence everyone desperately needed.

"Your sister is right," Harriet readily agreed. "After all, the top bridal magazines don't call her the premier event planner in New York for no reason. She'll think of something."

This news seemed to brighten the mood of everyone save for Olivia. While their spirits rose, she fought the urge to sink beneath the table.

The magazines *used* to call her that....

Before she lost her business.

Yet another secret she'd have to keep buried.

*W*restling with his thoughts, Reed turned down the dirt road heading home. He didn't feel right dwelling on his history with a married woman and needed a distraction.

He glanced out the window as he approached his mother's house, grateful when he spotted her reclining in a lounge chair on the front lawn.

The image could have been plucked from a flyer advertising vacations to the English countryside. Quaint and cozy, the charming stone structure resembled a storybook cottage, complete with lush ivy ambling up the exterior, a vibrant English garden, and creaking picket fence. He had fond memories of his childhood, roughhousing with his younger brother, Mark, while his mother warned them not to knock over her easels.

Since they'd moved out, and his father left, the tiny cottage had become even more cramped with his mother's art projects, be it landscape paintings or pottery. But Joan Hollis had become a well-known name in the artist community and she made a decent living off of her work.

Plus, it seemed to make her happy.

Or, as happy as she could be, all things considered.

He rolled to a stop when she waved.

"Care for a nightcap?" She raised the clay mug she'd made in her own kiln.

He put his van in park and hopped out, eager to take his mind off Olivia.

As he settled on the adjacent wicker lounge chair, Joan ducked inside.

A few minutes later, she returned with another handmade mug.

Steam curled from the rim, and Reed inhaled the earthy aroma. His mother's version of a nightcap consisted of strong valerian tea with a splash of warm milk and local wildflower honey.

They sat in comfortable silence for a few moments, sipping the soothing beverage as they listened to the gentle chirp of the evening's first chorus of crickets.

Reed was just starting to relax when Joan announced, "I heard Olivia's back in town."

He sputtered, spraying hot tea all over his lap. "News travels fast," he mumbled, wiping his mouth with the back of his hand.

"Have you seen her?"

"I had dinner at the Parkers' tonight."

Joan's eyes widened. "Really?"

Harriet's cold demeanor toward their family wasn't exactly a secret, and Joan's love and acceptance of Olivia's curious, unfettered nature hadn't helped the situation. When Olivia came over to play, Joan let her run wild, which often included climbing trees and tilling the garden with her bare hands. This didn't sit well with Harriet, who had strict rules about how a young lady ought to behave.

"I still find it hard to believe, myself," Reed admitted.

"How was it?" Joan asked, eyeing him closely.

"It was good. Baked chicken, mashed potatoes—"

"No!" she interrupted, exasperated. "I meant what was it like seeing Olivia again? She hasn't been home since well before her wedding. How many years has she been married now?"

"Four," Reed blurted. Realizing his mistake, he quickly added, "Maybe. Hard to say for sure."

His mother took a slow sip of tea, but he felt her gaze boring into him.

"Whatever happened between you two?"

"What do you mean?" Although a cool breeze rustled the lilac branches, dispersing their sweet scent, Reed felt uncomfortably warm all of a sudden.

"I always thought you two would wind up together."

"We were just friends."

She snorted. "Keep telling yourself that, if you must. But sooner or later, you'll have to move on, honey. And learn to love someone new."

"Because it's so easy?" he murmured, staring into his mug.

"No," she said softly. "I suppose it's not."

Hearing the pain in her voice, he glanced up and met her gaze. "I'm sorry, Mom. I shouldn't have said that."

"No, no. You're right. I need to practice what I preach." She tucked a wayward strand of hair behind her ear and offered a faint smile.

In the dim porch light, he could barely make out the silver streaks highlighting her dark, unruly waves. She usually gathered them in a messy bun, held in place with well-used paintbrushes or charcoal pencils. But tonight, she let them graze her shoulders.

As she smiled, deep creases appeared in the corners of her brown eyes, but they held the same sparkle from her youth. A few years into her sixties, she was still a beautiful woman. And whenever Reed thought about his father's affair, and the toll it had taken on her self-esteem, his blood heated.

Impulsively, he reached for her hand and gave it a squeeze. "Love you, Mom."

"Love you, too, honey."

They continued to sip their tea in silence.

How could he tell his mother that pining over Olivia was only part of the reason he never wanted to get married?

Admitting the demise of their marriage had rattled his faith in the institution would only add to her grief.

CHAPTER FOUR

$\mathcal{A}$s Olivia strolled down Main Street, an unexpected longing stirred in her heart.

She watched as Mac Houston, owner of the mercantile, arranged fresh produce in colorful baskets in front of his shop and a group of women chatted animatedly outside the Buttercup Bistro while their children played a rambunctious game of tag in the town square.

Life seemed simpler here. Sweeter, even. Many of the kids she'd known growing up never moved away and opened their own shops and businesses in town.

Countless times over the last few years, she'd wondered what her life would be like if she'd never left Poppy Creek. And more often than she wanted to admit, she felt a tiny pang of regret that she'd never become a part of the close-knit community the way Grant had.

Her brother made friends easily and had started dating Eliza shortly after moving to town. While the kids her age had tried to befriend her, she'd rebuffed their attempts, too afraid to risk getting close to anyone. Especially other girls.

After enduring years of bullying in a small private school in

New York, she'd learned to distrust a friendly smile. Eventually, the insincere friendships had turned to name-calling behind her back, then straight to her face. The cleverest tormentors came up with creative gems like Uglivia and Olivia Porker, while others resorted to more crass monikers. The cruelty had escalated from there.

She cringed at the painful memories.

The experience had made her closed off and suspicious, not letting anyone into her sphere of safety.

Except for Reed.

There had been something about his quiet, unobtrusive nature that put her at ease. He never pried. He never pushed. He simply let her be... *her.*

Lost in her thoughts, Olivia instinctively stopped in front of an old brick building that used to be Maggie's Place, a cozy bakery renowned for its jumbo-sized cinnamon rolls. Although the same sugary scent wafted from inside, the sign now read The Calendar Café.

While Grant had mentioned that Eliza took over the bakery after Maggie retired, she wasn't prepared for how much it had changed. The faded pink awning had been replaced by a newer one with cheerful yellow stripes. Vibrant red zinnias sprang from planter boxes lining the wide picture windows. The brick exterior, formerly painted an unappealing shade reminiscent of a certain stomach medication, now gleamed a soft antique white.

Curious about the improvements to the interior, she pushed through the front door, immediately welcomed by the mouthwatering aroma of buttery pastries and freshly brewed coffee.

The inviting, homey space bustled with activity as townsfolk ordered hot scones and specialty lattes while contented customers filled the comfy booths and tables, savoring their selections.

Olivia chose a bistro table by the window, hoping to recenter her frame of mind before meeting with Eliza. She'd come to discuss wedding details, but the wave of nostalgia and self-reflection caught her by surprise, derailing her train of thought.

As if regaining her footing after a divorce wasn't hard enough, being back home only added to her confusion.

"Hi! You must be Olivia." A soft-spoken brunette wearing a red apron and a warm, open smile stood by her table holding a steaming beverage. "I'm Cassie. Eliza told me you'd be stopping by." She set the tall glass on the table, scooting it toward her. "I made an educated guess based on what Eliza and Grant have told me about you. I hope you like it."

Olivia stared at the scrumptious-looking concoction in surprise. It smelled heavenly and she detected the faintest whiff of lavender. "What is it?"

"It's new. I'm thinking of calling it a White Rose and Lavender Mocha."

Intrigued by the unusual name, Olivia brought the rim to her lips and took a tentative sip. Notes of creamy white chocolate and velvety espresso swirled with the subtle and sweet undertones of rose and lavender.

"What do you think?" Cassie asked, glowing with hopeful expectation.

"Honestly? It's the best thing I've ever tasted." She took another sip, letting it warm the back of her throat.

The coffee shop she and Steven had frequented didn't serve anything that remotely compared to what she'd just tasted. And now that she'd experienced what coffee *could* taste like, she wouldn't miss their familiar haunt, which he'd claimed in the divorce. As if she'd even want to run into him anyway. Especially if he was with—

"I'm so glad you like it!" Cassie beamed, interrupting her melancholy musing.

"What'd you make?" Eliza asked, seamlessly slipping into their conversation.

"Something brand new I just whipped up."

"I'm not surprised." With a knowing smile, Eliza slid onto the chair across from Olivia. "Cassie has this knack for knowing exactly what kind of coffee someone will like. It's spooky."

Cassie laughed. "She's exaggerating. But I'm really glad you like it. And I'm so glad you're here to help with the wedding. I'm afraid I'm not doing a very good job as maid of honor."

"Don't be ridiculous! You've been beyond amazing," Eliza assured her. "It's not your fault the venue didn't work out."

As the women chatted, Olivia looked on in amazement. They seemed so loving and supportive of one another—so unlike any female friendship she'd ever witnessed. Her friends in New York had deserted her shortly after the divorce, affirming her worst fear—that she had nothing to offer on her own.

She'd tried to console herself with the reminder that Steven was the one who had all the wealth and connections, so of course they'd taken his side. But no matter how she'd tried to rationalize it, the betrayals didn't sting any less.

"Speaking of the venue," Cassie said thoughtfully. "I had an idea. But I'm not sure it's a good one."

"We'll take any suggestions at this point," Eliza told her.

"What about the Windsor Place?"

Eliza scrunched her nose, clearly not in love with the idea.

"The Windsor Place?" Olivia asked, unfamiliar with the name.

"Our friends are turning an abandoned property into a luxury inn," Eliza explained. "We call it the Windsor Place because it's on Windsor Lane and they haven't come up with a name for the inn yet. It would definitely have enough space, but it's awfully run-down, Cass."

"True, it still needs a lot of work," Cassie admitted. "But I saw Kat this morning and she said most of the kitchen is up and running, which is good news for the caterers. And Reed's landscaping the backyard, so you know it'll be beautiful. In fact, he and Lucy are out there today if you want to swing by and take a look."

Olivia straightened. Lucy? Who's Lucy?

"I suppose it's worth a look," Eliza relented. "But I have a million special orders today." She turned to Olivia. "Do you have time? If you say it'll work, then I'm on board."

"I'd love to check it out."

Both the venue *and* this Lucy person.

*R*eed jabbed his trowel into the topsoil a little harder than necessary.

He'd barely slept all night, too distracted by Olivia's presence in Poppy Creek.

Not to mention his mother's words.

I always thought you two would wind up together.

If he were honest, he'd pictured a life with Olivia, too. So much so, he'd flown to New York to surprise her on graduation day.

Except, he'd been the one surprised.

"Reed?"

He jumped at the sound of his name, and Lucy laughed.

"Didn't mean to startle you," she snickered. "Do you have a minute? I could use an extra set of hands."

"Sure thing." He rose to his feet, briskly wiping his palms on his jeans, scattering flecks of dirt.

Ever since Lucy Gardener quit her job staging homes for her father's real estate company, she'd taken on her new career with gusto. Her brother Jack, who owned the Windsor Place, asked her to oversee the renovations of the inn and the interior design, requesting that every single detail honor the history of the Colonial Revival estate while also incorporating modern comforts.

The project had been slow going, so far, since the construction crew worked in between other clients. But in the last few months, the sprawling mansion had been rewired, had its plumbing updated, and boasted a brand-new roof.

Reed had been put in charge of landscaping all thirty acres. Luckily, a serene wooded area covered two-thirds of the property, and Jack had hired a separate crew to groom the trails leading to the creek. Their mutual friend, Luke Davis, constructed a handful of benches to place at the most scenic locations along the path, creating cozy spots for future guests to relax and enjoy nature.

Reed's main contribution would be the garden in the backyard. A showstopping sight he'd modeled after opulent manors in the English countryside—his most ambitious project to date.

Fortunately, Jack and Kat didn't plan on opening the inn until the fall, so he still had plenty of time.

As Lucy led the way into an elegant sitting room with a large bay window and ornate, open-hearth fireplace, Reed marveled at the impressive architecture for the millionth time. He still couldn't get over the grandeur of the home, even amid the chaos of the renovations.

"I need your help measuring something," Lucy explained, stopping in front of a bare wall. "Penny found the most gorgeous antique sideboard, but I'm not sure it'll fit." She handed him one end of the measuring tape.

"Penny must be having a blast helping you furnish this place," Reed pointed out. Considering Penny Heart owned an antiques store in town, a project of this magnitude had to be a dream come true.

"Are you kidding?" Lucy grinned. "She's like a kid in a candy store. She probably sends me a hundred photos a day. But it's been great. I couldn't have better help. Especially since she's much more knowledgeable about all of the history, although I'm learning a lot." Bending down, she placed a Post-it on the ground, marking where the measuring tape ended.

"What are your plans when this place is up and running?"

"I never think that far ahead," she said with an infectious laugh. "I'm a *live-life-one-day-at-a-time* kind of girl."

She certainly exuded a laissez-faire aura, along with a vivacious personality and magnetic beauty. Reed knew several men who would hate to see her leave town, many of whom were on the Camden Construction crew. They couldn't seem to take their eyes off of her whenever she floated into the room. Which wasn't exactly safe considering most of them operated dangerous power tools.

But while he couldn't blame them, he never saw her in the same light.

For as long as he could remember, he'd only ever had eyes for one woman.

His thoughts flew to the secret project in his greenhouse. When it first began, he'd thought of it as a private homage, of sorts. It hadn't felt unseemly when Olivia was thousands of miles away on the other side of the continent.

But now, he wondered if he'd made a mistake.

At least she'd never find out about it.

CHAPTER FIVE

*A*s Olivia turned down Windsor Lane, she admired the tall sycamore trees lining the gravel road. But her subtle admiration quickly turned to disbelief when she reached the end of the circular driveway.

The most stunning home she'd ever seen came into view, stealing her attention like the tallest sunflower in a field of blooms.

She parked her rental car, taking a moment to soak in the breadth of its beauty.

The two-story brick structure boasted more windows than she could count, tall, stately columns, a grand entrance, and at least three chimneys. Although clearly under extensive renovations, it didn't take much imagination to picture it in full swing as a top-destination.

For a brief moment, she regretted that she wouldn't be around in the fall for the grand opening.

"Hello there." The cheerful, lilting voice pulled her from her thoughts and she spotted a striking young woman waving at her from the front porch. "When I heard a car approach, I thought the construction crew had arrived early today."

She skipped down the stone steps clad in designer jeans and a silky blouse Olivia recognized from an exclusive fashion line that hadn't been released to the general public yet.

This must be Lucy. Olivia immediately tensed, trying not to unfairly compare this woman to the girls who'd teased her in school, no matter how many similarities there might be on the surface.

"I heard you were back in town. Welcome home." The woman's broad smile radiated a familiarity Olivia hadn't expected. Did they know each other?

"I'm so sorry. Have we met before?" She felt her cheeks flush, embarrassed she didn't recognize her.

"I'm Lucy Gardener. I was a few grades behind you in school, so there's no reason you'd remember me."

"I still feel terrible. I'm awful with faces."

"Don't think a second more about it." Lucy shrugged it off with another breezy smile.

The effervescent blond possessed the kind of effortless confidence Olivia had always envied in other women. Even when she'd achieved what most people considered professional and personal success, she still didn't feel good enough, as though there was some unspoken rubric of self-worth, and she never quite matched up.

Putting aside her unwelcome insecurities, Olivia explained, "Cassie mentioned this might be a suitable venue for Grant and Eliza's wedding, so I thought I'd take a look. If that's okay."

"Of course! What a fantastic idea! There's certainly plenty of space."

"Luce, I—"

Olivia turned toward the familiar voice and saw Reed standing in the doorway, wide-eyed and speechless.

Her stomach tightened at the intimate way he'd truncated Lucy's name—the same way he used to shorten hers.

She immediately chided herself for the unfair—and

completely inappropriate—comparison. For the life of her, she couldn't understand these sudden bursts of irrational jealousy.

And she didn't like them. Not one bit.

"Reed, guess what?" Lucy gushed in excitement. "Olivia is here to see if the backyard would work for Grant and Eliza's wedding."

"Really?" Reed frowned. "As much as I'd like to help them find a new venue, I'm not sure I can have it up to Eliza's standards in only a few weeks."

Olivia instinctively switched to event-planner mode, not wanting to lose what could be their only viable venue. "What if I help?" she blurted impulsively.

Reed merely blinked in stunned silence.

"What a wonderful offer!" Lucy beamed, turning to Reed. "With Olivia's help, you could definitely have the backyard ready in time."

"I don't know...." His frown deepened, and Olivia's heartbeat stuttered.

She wasn't sure how she felt about working so closely together, but she was also out of venue ideas. A jumble of conflicting emotions, she held her breath, waiting for his final verdict.

"Please, Reed." Lucy clasped her hands together, gazing at him with a persuasive pout. "I'm confident it'll be spectacular. And I know it would mean the world to Eliza and Grant."

That seemed to assuage his doubts and his features softened. "I can't argue with that."

"Yay!" Lucy bounced on her toes, grinning brightly.

Reed chuckled. "Don't be too excited. Olivia still has to give it her seal of approval."

"Then I'll let you start the grand tour." After a friendly goodbye, she bounded back inside, leaving the two of them alone.

Reed made a sweeping gesture with his hand. "Shall we?"

As she fell in step beside him, she reminded herself that she should be happy for Reed and Lucy.

After all, she'd already had her shot at happily ever after.

And she'd failed—epically.

It was someone else's turn to try to beat the odds.

*a*s Olivia followed him to the backyard, Reed's pulse kicked into overdrive.

In a few minutes, she'd be entering his space, possibly the first of many times over the next few weeks.

He wasn't sure how he felt about the prospect of spending so much time with her.

Back when they'd hung out nearly every afternoon, they'd been kids. Sure, he'd cared about her, but it wasn't until she'd left for boarding school her sophomore year that he realized his feelings ran deeper.

They'd kept in touch and saw each other over the holidays, and when she returned home after high school graduation, he prayed she'd stay in Poppy Creek for good. He'd even planned to finally reveal how he felt about her.

Then she'd announced her acceptance to Columbia University. He'd been crushed but determined to support her decision.

The next four years were excruciating, and as her studies became more intense, they communicated less and less frequently. He'd known she'd dated here and there, but hadn't realized how serious one particular relationship had become.

Until he showed up to surprise her on the day of her graduation, which had turned into the worst moment of his life. His only consolation was that Olivia had no idea he'd been there... or what he'd had planned.

Clearing his throat—and his troubled thoughts—he asked, "So, what do you think?"

"I think..." Her gaze traveled the full expanse of the backyard. "I think it's perfect."

"You do?" He'd tried to see what she saw, but in his eyes, the space still needed a ton of work.

Although he'd managed to clear out all the weeds and bramble, revive the lawn, and laid a path of stepping stones from the back deck to the gazebo, he'd barely started planting the garden.

"This would make a beautiful aisle." She gestured toward the walkway. "We can arrange the chairs evenly on both sides." With her lips pursed thoughtfully, she traced a path toward the gazebo. "It could use a fresh coat of paint. But I love the intricate lattice and trim and the ornate cupola. It would look stunning wrapped in twinkle lights. Maybe a few hanging flower baskets and floral garlands draped here and twisted around here." Her eyes sparkling now, she pointed toward the posts and railings. "What do you think?"

"I think that would look great."

"What do you have planned for the rest of the yard?" She met his gaze, her expression emitting a contagious excitement.

"Well..." His heartbeat quickened. He had yet to share his landscape design with anyone, but he found himself eager to hear her thoughts. "See the small pond beneath the weeping willow? I plan to fill it with water lilies and plant blue irises along the east bank. And in this area over here, I want to create an intimate seating area surrounded by fragrant rosebushes in an assortment of colors and varieties. Over here, I envision hollyhocks, bellflowers, and daisies. While this area will have gladiolus, dahlias, and peonies. And lastly, we have the perfect spot for pansies, violas, and snapdragons." He'd almost left the last one off the list, knowing they were her favorite. But he couldn't imagine his design without them.

A pretty blush swept across her cheeks. "It sounds breathtaking."

Suddenly a little flustered, he strode toward the side of the house, putting some distance between them. "I also pruned the wisteria on the pergola over here, so it should be in full bloom by the wedding. The guests could enter underneath, through the side yard rather than going through the house, which will still be under renovations."

"I love it. Fantastic idea." She whipped out her phone and started typing notes with an exhilarated energy.

Every fiber in her being seemed to come alive, and in that moment, he realized she must truly love her job.

A conclusion that both pleased and saddened him.

She'd be leaving soon, returning to her life in New York... and to her husband.

"I have a few thoughts regarding wedding flowers," she said, glancing up from her screen. "Mind if I come by your nursery tomorrow to see what you have?"

"Not at all. Just give me a heads-up before you come over so I can make sure I'm not out in the field."

And give him plenty of time to hide his secret project.

CHAPTER SIX

*O*livia flopped onto her side, too restless to sleep. She'd gone to bed early, hoping slumber would put an end to her troubled thoughts, but they stubbornly persisted.

If anything, her confusion seemed more deafening in the silence.

After her divorce, she'd been bitter and angry. At God, Steven, and perhaps most of all, *herself*.

She'd vowed to never fall in love again. She didn't see the point. Why risk such excruciating pain a second time? Could a person even survive that much heartache more than once? She didn't think she could.

So, she really didn't understand the strange sensations she'd started to experience around Reed. The flutter of uncertainty in the pit of her stomach. The brief flicker of hope. The pangs of jealousy.

She didn't want any of it. Not when it complicated the one relationship in her life that had never caused her even an ounce of sadness.

Well, not sadness, per se. Disappointment, maybe.

There'd been a moment—once—when she'd thought Reed

might feel something more than friendship. She'd barely allowed herself to believe it was possible. After all, for years, she'd been a shy, awkward bundle of nerves. Certainly not someone Reed would ever consider dating.

When she'd announced her acceptance to Columbia, she'd hoped he would say she shouldn't go. But deep down, she knew that wasn't fair. He'd never done anything but support her. Why would that occasion be any different?

Slipping out of bed, she threw a light cardigan over her silky pajama set and tiptoed downstairs. She needed to visit the one place that always cleared her head.

As she crept down the hallway, the TV blared from the study. From the combined laughter, it sounded like both of her parents were watching *M*A*S*H* reruns. Olivia wasn't sure which she found more surprising—the fact that her parents were spending time together or that her mother had agreed to watch a television show based on the Korean War.

At least they wouldn't notice her duck outside.

The instant the crisp night air caressed her cheeks, a weight lifted from her shoulders.

Guided only by moonlight, she padded barefoot behind the house toward the creek, savoring the soothing sensation of her toes sinking into the cool grass. The gentle trickle of the stream kept her company as she made her way to a familiar footpath she'd traveled often as a child.

With all her heart, she hoped the tree house she and Reed had built on his parents' property her first summer in Poppy Creek still remained. While it more closely resembled a few planks stretched between the low-hung branches of an oak tree, it had quickly become her haven—a place to escape her troubles.

And she'd had more than her fair share at a young age.

Although she thought she'd left the bullies behind in New York, social media provided a means to hurl insults across the internet. Which is why, as an adult, she avoided the so-called social networks when it came to her private life, only utilizing them for her event-planning business. And she didn't even use that anymore.

In hindsight, her repulsion for displaying personal details online had offered an unexpected benefit. After the divorce, she hadn't needed to explain the conspicuous absence of Steven from her photos. Plus, her days mostly consisted of feeling sorry for herself, which didn't make for compelling entertainment.

As she approached the clearing—spurred on by muscle memory—she slowed when she caught sight of twinkling lights through the trees.

Halting abruptly, she gaped in complete awe at the sight of a sprawling tree house several feet above the ground.

Nothing like the primitive structure they'd constructed as kids, it boasted a two-tier deck, grand staircase, and ingenious pulley system.

Clearly, this wasn't a child's fort or playhouse.

Someone lived here. But who? As far as she knew, Bruce and Joan Hollis still owned the property.

For a moment, her thoughts flew to Reed. They used to fantasize about building a live-in tree house to rival the Swiss Family Robinson home from the 1960s film.

Was it possible he'd actually followed through on their childhood dream?

She approached the bottom of the staircase and called out, "Hello? Anybody home?"

A muffled voice responded, "Hello!"

Tentatively, she climbed a few more steps. "I don't mean to intrude, but I've never seen anything quite like your beautiful home. May I come up?"

"Come up!" the strange voice called back, almost as if it were mimicking her words.

Uncertain if the owner was inviting her inside, she ascended the rest of the way and knocked on the front door.

"Come in!" came the shrill command.

Before she could change her mind, Olivia turned the knob and pushed the door open, dying to know who she'd find on the other side.

*R*eed shut off the shower and wrapped a towel around his waist, smiling in amusement. Through the gentle cascade of water, he thought he heard his cockatiel talking to himself. "Nips, what are you babbling about?" he chuckled as he stepped out of the bathroom.

He immediately froze.

Olivia stood in the doorway, her features pallid as she stared in shock.

"Olivia?"

"I'm so sorry! I-I-I'll go." With a mortified expression, she turned abruptly and smacked her head on the doorjamb.

Forgetting he was clad in nothing more than a towel, he rushed to her side. "Are you all right?"

"I'm fine," she groaned, covering her forehead—and her eyes—with both hands.

"Come on. Sit down. I'll get you some ice." He led her toward the couch before realizing he should probably put some pants on first. "I'll be right back. Don't move." He ducked inside his bedroom and threw on a pair of sweats and a T-shirt.

When he returned to the living room, his heart vaulted into his throat at the sight of Nips perched on Olivia's shoulder. "Careful! Nips doesn't like strangers. He'll take a big chunk out of your ear."

"You think so?" Olivia purred as the brightly colored cockatiel nuzzled her cheek, clearly putting her at ease. "He seems like a total sweetie pie to me."

Reed balked. He'd never seen Nips take to anyone so quickly

before. "I guess I stand corrected." Still baffled, he strode to the kitchen to fill a Ziploc bag with ice.

"Is that how he got his name? From nipping people?" she asked, stroking the top of his feathery head with her fingertip.

"That and I named him after the monkey in *Swiss Family Robinson*."

"I guess he is kind of a mischievous monkey," she said with a laugh. "You know he invited me inside?"

"What a rascal." Reed grinned, secretly glad he had. He'd have to remember to give him a small piece of dried papaya as a treat later.

After settling beside Olivia on the couch, he handed her the bag of ice and a kitchen towel. "Hold this on your forehead. You're going to have a decent bump in the morning."

She didn't seem to hear him, too engrossed with studying the tree house.

He'd often fantasized about the first time she saw it, but he had to admit, stepping out of the shower and nearly giving her a concussion didn't come close to what he'd imagined.

"You like it?" he asked, watching her expression.

"Reed, it's… unbelievable," she breathed, her gaze traveling from the loft bedroom to the branches springing through the floorboards to the river rock fireplace. "You did it. You actually built our dream house."

His pulse quickened when she said "our dream house." She had no idea that he'd actually had her in mind when he'd sketched out the initial design. "Technically, I didn't build it. There's a team of guys in Lupine Ridge that travel the country building these for a living. But a lot of the design elements were my idea. My favorite is the skylight above the bed with a retractable shade. I love falling asleep gazing at the stars through a canopy of trees."

"That sounds heavenly. And I hate to say it, but it's way better than our measly two-by-fours nailed to a few branches. I don't blame you for upgrading."

"Can you stand? I'd like to show you something." He stood and held out his hand for Nips, who hopped onto his finger. "But first, time to relocate this scalawag." After setting him on a perch, he whispered, "Good boy," in a tone low enough that Olivia couldn't overhear him.

"Other than the sore spot on my head, I feel fine." She set the bag of ice on the coffee table and followed him to the window.

"Look down there." He pointed below to a platform of pine boards illuminated by a string of bistro lights.

Her face lit up. "You kept it! You actually kept our pathetic little tree house," she laughed.

"Hey, we had some pretty good times in that tree house," he protested with a teasing grin. "And it's still yours, anytime you need a place to think."

He thought she'd be pleased by the offer, but a somber shadow crossed her features. "I'm so sorry, Reed," she murmured softly.

"Sorry? For what?"

"For losing touch. For letting our friendship fade. For... not calling you back at Christmas." She met his gaze, her expression hesitant and uncertain. "I don't deserve it, but I hope you can forgive me for being such a terrible friend."

For a moment, Reed didn't know what to say. Forgive her? He'd never felt anything negative toward her. Unless he counted missing her so badly, he could barely breathe.

"It happens. Friends lose touch sometimes. But you're back now. For a few more weeks, at least." He tried to sound cheerful, although the thought of her leaving again filled him with conflicting emotions.

"That's true." She smiled. "And I plan on making the most of them. I'd love to get together with your parents while I'm in town."

Darn. She didn't know. That was the downside to Olivia not using social media. Although, he'd been grateful not to constantly be bombarded with images of her perfect life with Steven.

As he mulled over how to best spill the bad news, he decided to take the direct approach. "Mom would love to see you. But Dad... he, uh, lives at the coast now."

The color drained from her rosy complexion. "Your parents split up?"

"Yeah, a few years ago."

"I—" She paused, as though collecting her thoughts. She seemed to be taking the news almost as hard as he had. "I don't know what to say. Except that I'm so incredibly sorry to hear that." Her voice cracked slightly, and her eyes glistened.

"It's okay. These things happen." Probably the feeblest thing he could have said, but he was desperate to put a smile back on her face. "Do you have some time? We could watch a movie or something. Nips is clearly eager for you to stay."

He nodded toward the perch where the yellow-faced scamp bobbed back and forth in an effort to get their attention.

The tiniest of smiles pulled at the edge of her mouth, but she shook her head. "I'd love to, but I should get back. No one knows I left the house. But I'll see you tomorrow." She stopped to say goodbye to Nips on her way out, rubbing the nape of his neck.

The little bird closed his eyes, soaking up the attention.

Apparently, Reed wasn't the only one who'd fallen hard for Olivia Parker.

CHAPTER SEVEN

*A*s Olivia wound along the scenic country road, she took a languid sip from her to-go cup before nestling it back in the recessed holder.

After a restless night, she'd stopped by The Calendar Café for one of Cassie's special mochas before heading to Reed's nursery.

No matter how hard she tried, she couldn't shake the image of Reed's tree house—or what it meant. Growing up, it had been a joint dream. Should she read into the fact that he'd made it a reality? Or did he simply like tree houses and it had nothing to do with the countless hours they'd spent together imagining every detail?

The question circled in her mind on an endless loop, occasionally complicated by the news about his parents' divorce.

The startling revelation had hit too close to home, for more reasons than one.

Joan and Bruce Hollis had seemed like the perfect couple— loving, happy, and embarrassingly affectionate, everything her parents hadn't been.

Even as a young girl, if someone had asked her whose parents would be more likely to split—hers or Reed's—she wouldn't have hesitated to predict hers.

But as she'd recently learned, life rarely turned out the way you thought it would.

Her parents' marriage had never seemed stronger.

While hers...

A solitary tear slid down her cheek and she roughly wiped it away as she approached the entrance to Reed's nursery.

Today, she wanted to put all unpleasant memories aside. With the bright, cheerful sun shimmering in the clear blue sky, she couldn't have asked for a more glorious afternoon.

Determined to savor every detail, she lowered all four windows, letting the wind whip her hair around her neck and shoulders. She didn't even mind when the wheels kicked up dust along the dirt road. In fact, she relished the earthy scent.

Her blissful mood momentarily faltered when she passed the sign for Sanders Farm, which abutted Reed's property, but she quickly pushed the thought aside. That was a problem for another day.

Instead, she looked ahead to the wooden archway that acted as a picture frame to the brilliant blooms just beyond. Vibrant reds, yellows, purples, and blues stretched on for miles, like a rainbow come to earth.

As she parked beside Reed's VW van, she fixed her gaze on an arresting glass-and-metal structure jutting from the sea of vivid colors. With its ornate iron framework tinted a stunning pale green from oxidation and the plethora of glass windows glinting in the sunlight, the stunning Victorian-era greenhouse commanded as much attention as the surrounding flowers.

If she were Eliza, she'd want to get married here. Of course, that would mean cutting a few hundred people off the guest list since nearly every speck of land belonged to the flora, be it roses, zinnia, cosmos, sunflowers, or a dozen or so other varieties.

Reed must have heard her arrive because a few seconds later, he emerged from the greenhouse.

As he strode toward her, she momentarily forgot how to unbuckle a seat belt.

Somehow, Reed made faded jeans and a leather gardening belt look more attractive than a Dolce & Gabbana suit. And the tanned, muscled forearms with streaks of dirt did not detract from the appeal, either.

"Hey, Liv! Welcome to my home away from home."

As the nickname rolled off his tongue, goose bumps scattered across her arms. She hadn't been sure she'd ever hear him call her Liv again. And she found the sound both comforting and exhilarating.

"If I didn't know your other home was a tree house, I wouldn't understand how you could ever leave this place."

He grinned, appearing pleased with her compliment. "Where would you like to start the tour?"

"Definitely the greenhouse." From the second she spotted the beguiling building, it called to her like a treasure chest waiting to be explored.

"After you." He swung open the heavy iron-and-glass door and gestured for her to step inside.

Immediately upon entering, Olivia observed the shift in temperature. Though it was hotter, it wasn't unpleasant. Knowing Reed, he'd added excellent ventilation.

As she followed him through the neat rows of planter boxes and seedling trays, she noticed the way he came alive in the space. His dark eyes brightened as he showcased his favorite blooms, and the adorable giddy smile never left his face.

An infectious energy rippled through the expansive space, and coupled with the intoxicating scent of warm potting soil and sweet-smelling freesias and gardenias, Olivia felt oddly invigorated. She couldn't wait to get her hands dirty.

She paused in front of a large pot containing a single rosebush. Impulsively, she caressed the velvety, lavender-hued petals with silvery undertones. "The Sterling Silver rose was always my favorite rose."

"I remember." His voice carried a note of tender nostalgia that sent a shiver down her spine.

Which she promptly ignored.

"Too bad Eliza's wedding colors don't include purple. These would be lovely in a bouquet."

"What are her wedding colors?"

"Pink and a soft, antique blue. You don't happen to have any blue roses, do you?" she asked, quickly adding, "I realize blue roses don't occur naturally, but you can dye the roots, right?"

He hesitated a moment before answering, "You can. But I don't have any."

"That's a shame. I suppose we can go with pink. Although, the blue would have a little more pizzazz."

"I know where we can get some, if you have time for a field trip tomorrow."

She met his gaze and the unwelcome flutter in her stomach returned.

A field trip would mean time alone in the car together. Certainly not the best idea in the world.

It's for Grant and Eliza, she reminded herself before agreeing to Reed's proposal.

Although, deep down, she knew that wasn't the only reason she'd said yes.

*a*s Reed guided Olivia out of the greenhouse, his heart plummeted when she paused and pointed toward the far right-hand corner.

"What's back there?" She peered curiously at a white tarp draped like a curtain and surrounded by tall palms.

He racked his brain for a reasonable answer other than *a secret project I don't want you to see.* "It's some broken pots and random scraps I need to get rid of but haven't had time."

Okay, so not a blatant lie. Those were all true. He just failed to mention the other item hiding among them.

Luckily, she seemed satisfied with his response and followed him outside without pressing further.

"I think I saw some pink zinnias when I drove in. Can we take a look?"

"You can check out anything you want." *Except for what's behind the tarp.*

As they strode toward the row of perky pink blooms, his phone buzzed in his back pocket. "It's my mom," he said glancing at the screen.

"You should never ignore your mother," she warned with a teasing grin.

"Good point," he chuckled, accepting the call. "Hey, Mom. What's up?"

"What are your plans for dinner tonight?"

"I'll probably pick up a burger from Jack's. Why?"

"Wrong. You're coming over to my place."

"Okay...." He found the adamant invitation odd considering they'd already had dinner that week.

"And you're bringing Olivia with you," she added matter-of-factly.

He suppressed an eye roll at his mother's blatant manipulation. "How do you know she doesn't have plans?"

"Is she there? Put me on speaker."

Reed instantly regretted telling her that Olivia would be coming by the nursery that afternoon.

He mouthed the words *I'm sorry* before pressing the speaker button.

"Olivia! Hi, honey. Are you having a good time?"

As realization settled across Olivia's features, she flashed him another grin. "Hi, Mrs. Hollis. Yes, Reed's nursery is beautiful."

"Oh, honey. Call me Joan. You're a grown woman now. No need for the formality. What are you doing tonight?"

"Well, I—"

"You're coming to my house for dinner," Joan cut in. "I haven't seen you in years, and I won't take no for an answer."

Reed barely avoided a groan of embarrassment.

"I'd love to," Olivia said, her eyes sparkling. She appeared to be biting back a laugh.

He tried to whisper that she didn't have to give in to his mother's demands, but she waved away his concern and asked, "What time?"

"Oh, about five thirty, six o'clock," Joan said casually. "I'll leave the tofu casserole warming in the oven for whenever you arrive."

Typical. His mother could never stick to a normal schedule.

"Do you still like mochi? I found some made with mango jam that's to die for."

This time, Olivia couldn't contain her giggle. "Sounds delicious."

"Fabulous! See you tonight. Kisses to you both." And with that, his mother ended the call.

"Sorry about that." Reed gruffly stuffed the phone back inside his pocket.

"Don't be. I love your mother. And I was just saying last night how much I'd like to see her."

"True. But have you forgotten she can't cook?"

"She *can* cook. You just don't like tofu," Olivia corrected with a playful smirk. "I still remember your dad sneaking chocolate syrup in those healthy smoothies she used to make us after school."

Reed laughed at the memory, then immediately sobered. When it came to what constituted healthy eating, his parents never saw eye to eye. Had that been one of the many red flags he'd missed?

"I'm so sorry, Reed," Olivia said softly. "I shouldn't have mentioned it."

"It's okay. It's not anything you said. It's just... sometimes I wonder if I should have seen my parents' divorce coming. I feel like the worst son in the world for not noticing the warning signs."

"You'd be surprised what people miss," she murmured, her gaze fixed on the ground.

Something in her voice made him wonder if someone close to her had gone through a similar experience. Perhaps a friend, or maybe even Steven's parents.

The truth was, divorce was depressingly common.

Another reason avoiding marriage altogether seemed like the wisest decision.

CHAPTER EIGHT

a smile teased the corner of Olivia's mouth as she ambled along the narrow footpath, guided by the gentle breeze rustling the dogwood branches. As if bidding a final farewell, the setting sun bestowed a breathtaking sheen across the field of wildflowers, gilding each petal in gold.

On impulse, she stopped and removed her sandals, digging her toes into the cool earth.

In New York, the only time she went barefoot was inside her own home. And even then, Steven preferred to see her in high heels.

As she passed Reed's tree house on the way to Joan's cottage, she stole a quick glance. It looked even more magical in the shimmering twilight, and she couldn't help wondering what it would be like to live there.

"Hey! Care for a walking buddy?" Reed called out cheerily as he descended the staircase. He'd changed into a clean pair of jeans and a pale-blue button-down that complemented his tanned skin.

"Of course." Her stomach performed its irritating backflip routine again.

As he joined her on the trail, he glanced down at her bare feet and flashed an amused grin.

Heat swept across her cheeks. "I was going to put my shoes back on before we got there."

"Why? You know what Mom always says."

"Bare feet keep us grounded," she recited with a laugh.

"Exactly."

They fell in step, traversing the path in comfortable silence, enjoying the bullfrogs that decided to serenade the rest of their short journey.

She'd almost forgotten how much she missed the peaceful serenity of the countryside. While she appreciated human design and ingenuity, nothing compared to the beauty of God's creation.

She would miss it when she headed back to the city.

For the first time since her arrival, an unexpected thought crossed her mind.

Did she have to go back? What was left for her in New York? Her entire life had been obliterated right before her eyes. Was it possible she could start over in Poppy Creek?

Of course, if she did, she'd have to admit to everyone her long list of failures....

A familiar cottage came into view, pushing the idea to the back of her mind.

"It looks even more charming than I remembered," she breathed, pausing at the tiny wooden gate that hung ajar.

The flowers in particular appeared lush and more vibrant, which oddly gave her hope. If Joan could thrive after her divorce, then perhaps so could she.

"Did you remember to eat beforehand?" Reed asked in jest as they entered the garden.

"And be too full for the tofu casserole?" she teased, bending down to slip on her sandals.

"Don't bother," Joan called from the doorway. "You know my

philosophy around here." She wiggled her bare toes, and Olivia giggled.

If possible, Joan had become even more beautiful over the years. She wore billowy, bohemian-style pants and a crochet cardigan that swept down to her ankles. With her wavy hair twisted into a loose bun held in place by paintbrushes, her dark, sparkling eyes stole the show—the same eyes Bruce used to say perpetually held a laugh, just waiting for him to coax it from hiding.

Used to say...

She would have to remember to avoid any mention of Bruce.

"Welcome home, dear." Joan opened her arms, and Olivia stepped into her embrace, momentarily lost in her comforting earthy scent of fresh herbs and potter's clay.

As they pulled apart, she thought Joan's eyes looked mistier than before.

"I'm sorry, ladies." Reed glanced up from his phone. "I won't be able to stay for dinner. Flower emergency."

"Flower emergency?" Olivia repeated, skeptical any such thing existed.

"Pastor Bellman forgot his anniversary and needs a bouquet of irises delivered as soon as possible or his next sermon will have to be on forgiveness."

Joan slipped her arm through Olivia's, perfectly content with the change in plans. "That just means we'll have a chance for some girl talk."

Worried that would mean discussing Steven, Olivia watched Reed head back down the path with nervous trepidation.

But Joan didn't seem to notice as she blithely ushered her inside.

The second Olivia crossed the threshold, pleasant memories swept over her. The smell of acrylic paint still permeated the air and canvases in various stages of completion filled every nook and cranny.

When they finally reached the cozy kitchen, the aroma of garlic, rosemary, and thyme flooded her senses, and Joan went straight to the oven to remove a freshly baked baguette. Wisps of steam curled from the golden crust as she set it on the butcher-block island. "Have a seat, dear. You remember how it works in this house."

With a smile, she settled at the rustic farm table while Joan uncorked a bottle of elderberry wine. "I don't remember ever having wine," Olivia teased.

Although, she had always loved Joan's special brand of hospitality, which invited every single person who entered her home treat it as if it were their own.

"Now that you're grown, I thought we could share our first glass together." Her tone held a weightiness that Olivia wasn't expecting. And as Joan slid the glass toward her, she took the seat opposite and asked softly, "How long has it been?"

"Since what?" Unsuspecting, Olivia took a sip of wine, tasting hints of blackberry and cherry in the sweet, syrupy drink.

"Since the divorce."

Sputtering in surprise, Olivia set down her glass. "What?"

"I'm sorry, dear. Perhaps I should have been more subtle." Joan passed her a napkin.

Dabbing the droplets of wine from her chin, she asked, "How did you know?"

"I can see it in your eyes, honey. The eyes are the canvas of the soul. Your entire life is painted there, if one knows how to look."

Uncertain how to respond, Olivia continued blotting her face.

"So," Joan tried again. "How long has it been?"

With a resigned sigh, she answered honestly, "We've been separated almost a year. The divorce itself only took three months. Steven's lawyer called New York's divorce process quick and painless, especially if you agree on the division of assets. Turns out, he was only right about the *quick* part."

"I'm so sorry." Joan reached across the table and squeezed her hand.

As tears sprang to her eyes, Olivia murmured a *thank you* past the lump in her throat.

"Does Reed know?"

She shook her head. "I didn't want anyone to know. At least, not until after the wedding."

"I see." Joan contemplated this a moment. "While I think secrets are rarely a good idea, I suppose I can understand your desire to wait. Divorce tends to have a ripple effect."

"More like a tsunami," Olivia muttered with a wry smile.

"It's a good sign that you're able to find humor, even when it hurts."

"Is that how you learned to cope with it?" Olivia asked gently, adding, "Reed told me about you and Bruce."

"I figured he might."

"How long has it been for you?"

"Two and a half years too long."

Surprised by the strain in Joan's voice, she asked, "You still miss him?"

"Every day, I'm afraid."

Taken aback, Olivia sat in stunned silence, trying to process Joan's admission.

"I suppose you expected me to say that I've moved on by now?"

"I—" Olivia faltered, not sure how to answer that.

"It's all right, honey." Joan mustered a small smile. "Somedays, I wish I could move on. Love is a funny thing, isn't it? How we can be angry and miss someone at the same time."

Olivia wished she could relate, but she didn't feel either of those emotions anymore. "May I ask what happened?"

"You can. But I'm afraid I'm not the one with those answers. The divorce wasn't my decision."

"It wasn't mine, either," Olivia admitted, barely above a whisper. To her horror, tears stung her eyes again.

"Do you miss Steven?"

Olivia stared at her hands tightly wound in her lap, her cheeks hot with shame. "Truthfully? No, I don't." She forced herself to meet Joan's gaze. "I never wanted a divorce. And I still mourn the loss of my marriage. But I can't honestly say that I miss him. And I'm worried..." She bit her bottom lip, wavering over her next words. "I'm worried that means I'm broken. That there must be something wrong with me."

The tears she'd been suppressing suddenly broke free, slipping from the corner of her eye.

Joan leaned forward and placed both hands over hers. "Do you know why I've always found it fitting that snapdragons are your favorite flower?"

"No." Olivia sniffled, confused by the change in topic.

"Because snapdragons represent grace and strength, two qualities you possess in spades. You may feel broken now. But trust me, you're going to get through this even stronger than you were before."

Olivia wasn't sure she believed her, but she appreciated the sentiment. "Thank you." Ignoring the wine stains on her napkin, she dried her tears.

"What do you think about skipping the casserole and going straight for dessert?" Joan asked, rising from her chair.

"I'd like that very much."

"Then dessert it is. There's just one more thing." With a meaningful glance, she added, "You should tell Reed."

*I*rises in hand, Reed knocked on Pastor Bellman's front door, as instructed.

To his surprise, Betsy Bellman answered wearing an apron that read, *Man doesn't live on bread alone. He also needs butter.*

"Hello, darlin'. Aren't those the prettiest flowers I ever did see." Even after more than a decade in Poppy Creek, her Southern accent shone through. So did her ever-present smile. She had to be one of the sunniest people he'd ever met.

But he hadn't expected to see her tonight. Had he inadvertently ruined Pastor Bellman's surprise?

"Oh, sweetie. You look about as lost as last year's Easter egg. Is something wrong?"

"No, ma'am. I just thought…" How could he explain his last-minute delivery without revealing that Pastor Bellman had forgotten their anniversary?

"Let me guess." She smiled sweetly. "You're here because Hugh forgot our anniversary."

"Uh…" Words continued to fail him.

She laughed, her green eyes crinkling as her full cheeks grew even rounder. "Oh, bless your little heart. If I had a flower for every time he forgot our anniversary… Well, *I'd* be the one with the flower farm."

Just then, Pastor Bellman emerged from his study, clearly startled. "Sweetheart, I thought you said you were running to the store for some butter?"

"I found some in the freezer. And look what else I found." She gestured toward the deep violet blooms still gripped in Reed's hands.

He had to admit, he found the exchange quite fascinating. Betsy didn't seem the slightest bit irked.

"You caught me." Hugh grinned sheepishly. "I'm sorry, Bets. I really don't have a good excuse." He planted a kiss on her cheek. "Can I make it up to you?"

"These flowers are a start." She finally reached for the bouquet and nuzzled her nose in the soft petals. "Mmm, they smell exactly like my mama's chocolate cake."

Hugh reached into his back pocket for his wallet, but Reed waved his hand aside. "It's my anniversary gift to you two. How many years has it been?"

"Why thank you, son. It's been—" He glanced at his wife, who answered for him.

"Thirty-nine years."

"Wow." Reed whistled, unabashedly impressed. "That's quite a long time. What's your secret?"

"Buckets and buckets of prayer," Betsy laughed.

"My beautiful wife is never wrong." Hugh lovingly looped his arm around her waist. "And I'll let you in on another secret. A good marriage takes two things. Without them, you're in for an uphill battle."

"And what are those two things?" Reed asked, surprised by how badly he wanted to know.

"Love and grace. They go hand in hand. Having more love makes it easier to give someone grace. And having more grace makes it easier to love. When those two work together, you can weather any storm."

Although the pastor had a habit of mixing metaphors, his advice sounded solid.

With one exception….

What happened when one person in the marriage ran out of both?

CHAPTER NINE

*O*livia never thought she'd see the day when Sylvia Carter set foot in her mother's house.

Sylvia was a former Broadway actress and director of Poppy Creek's small theater group, and her dramatic, flamboyant nature vehemently clashed with Harriet's prim and proper disposition.

Not to mention, both women liked to be in charge.

However, their frivolous rivalry escalated the previous year when Sylvia's daughter, Eliza, revealed that Harriet had been blackmailing her into keeping the identity of Ben's father a secret to protect Grant's promising future.

While Olivia had plenty of experience dealing with her mother's controlling tendencies, Harriet had crossed a line, bordering on unforgivable.

And yet, Grant and Eliza had shown a level of love and forgiveness that transcended earthly understanding. And in the mirror of their kindness, Harriet finally faced the person she'd become.

If Olivia hadn't seen her mother's transformation with her own eyes, she wouldn't have believed it. In fact, she still had trouble accepting the startling change.

And even though Harriet was currently gardening in the backyard, she wouldn't blame Sylvia in the slightest for refusing to stop by.

"While I appreciate you doing this," Olivia told her, "I could have come to your house."

"Don't be silly." With an exaggerated flourish, Sylvia draped an assortment of Renaissance-style gowns across the plump couch cushions. "I had to drop off Reed's costume, anyway. Besides, your mother and I may not be a dynamic duo like Angela Lansbury and Bea Arthur, but we're not mortal enemies anymore."

"So, you've forgiven her, too?" Olivia asked, surprised by her forthrightness. There was something about Sylvia's spirited, outspoken personality that made her feel more forward than usual.

"Begrudgingly, at first. But yes, I did. Grant and Eliza wanted us to reconcile for the sake of the family." Sylvia perched on the arm of the couch, meeting her gaze with a candid expression. "To be perfectly honest, it helped to think of Ben and the kind of example I'd be setting. But you know what? Your mother has changed. Don't get me wrong, she's no Glinda. But she's not the Wicked Witch of the West, either. And I have faith that her growth is genuine."

Olivia smiled at the Broadway references, but she couldn't help a niggling question. "Do you ever wonder if having faith in people is... I don't know... foolish?"

"Perhaps, sometimes." She shrugged her shoulders, lifting her overly processed blond hair. "But the way I see it, there are only two things in life that will never let you down: the Good Lord and good lighting."

Sylvia's dark eyes glinted with humor, but then a shadow stole over them as she said in a more serious tone, "The rest takes faith. Is it scary? You betcha. Is it worth it? One hundred percent. Otherwise, life would be awfully lonely, don't you think?"

"I suppose you're right," Olivia said quietly, mulling over her words.

If she were honest, her own life was living proof. She could count on one hand the number of people she'd actually let past her carefully constructed walls. And even then, she still restricted access, not allowing them to see all of her scars and imperfections.

"Are you all right, doll? You look a million miles away."

Sylvia's concerned tone snapped Olivia from her reverie and she forced another smile. "Fine, thank you. Just trying to decide which dress to try on first." She directed her gaze to the pile of brocade and velvet.

"What did you say the costumes were for again?"

"The nursery we're visiting today is closed for a private event. A Shakespeare-themed wedding. But Reed's friend said she could get us in, if we blend in with the guests."

"Oh! Why didn't you say so?" Sylvia's dark eyes brightened. "I know just the one." Rummaging through the stack, she plucked a lavender-hued gown from the center of the mound. "This one is perfect. With your coloring, you'll be prettier than Juliet herself."

Mesmerized, Olivia grazed the delicate embroidery along the empire waistline. "It's beautiful."

"Try it on. I have a feeling it'll fit like a glove."

A few minutes later, after gingerly slipping the gown over her expertly curled ringlets, Olivia swept back into the room, stunned by her sudden surge in confidence. "I've worn countless evening gowns before, but this..." She swished the long skirt back and forth. "This feels different."

"Ah..." Sylvia flashed a knowing smirk. "You're experiencing the magic of a good wardrobe department, my dear. You slip into the perfect costume and you instantly become someone else. It's quite freeing, isn't it?"

"Now I see why you love acting so much."

"Like me, your beauty is born for the stage. You're like a young Elizabeth Taylor."

"Thanks," Olivia laughed. "But I think I'll leave the acting to you."

Although maybe the costume would help her muster the courage to finally tell Reed the truth.

*R*eed knew ogling Olivia wasn't his finest moment. But he wasn't prepared to see her walk out the front door in that dress.

He'd seen a lot of beautiful things in his life. Even a rare, rainbow-colored orchid.

But nothing could top the sight before him.

"Nice tights." Her eyes sparkled with laughter as she surveyed his ridiculous getup.

"Why, thank you, fair maiden." He tipped his feather-plumed hat.

While he'd never consider himself a fashion expert, it wasn't a stretch to say that designers in the sixteenth century had terrible taste.

Except for Olivia's outfit. She looked… Well, he couldn't quite put it into words. But he sure hoped Steven knew how lucky he was.

"Your carriage awaits, my lady." He opened the passenger door of his van and waited for her to climb inside before gently closing it behind her.

The entire drive to the nursery they chatted like old times, laughing and teasing each other like they were kids again.

It felt good. Great, actually.

Although he wasn't proud of it, he couldn't help wondering if that's what it would be like to be married to her. Of course, things wouldn't be a bed of roses all the time. They'd probably have their fair share of squabbles. But he suspected love and grace wouldn't be in short supply if Olivia was his wife. And as much as it pained him to admit, he hoped she and Steven had the kind of marriage Hugh and Betsy had.

For all of his own regrets, he wanted her to be happy.

When they pulled into the parking lot of Ciao Bella Garden, they exchanged an amused glance.

The entire nursery resembled a lively Renaissance faire, complete with a juggling court jester, lute musicians, and fire-breathers.

The parking attendant permitted them past the brocade rope, and they seamlessly blended into the rollicking crowd of wedding guests guzzling hard cider and chomping oversize turkey legs.

When one of the performers spewed a stream of fire mere inches from Olivia's face, she yelped in surprise, stumbling backward into Reed's arms.

His heart hammered against his chest as he held her during the split-second interaction, trying not to inhale the enticing floral scent of her shampoo.

Setting her back on her feet, he teased, "We should grab his business card in case Grant and Eliza want to add some entertainment to their wedding."

"I think I'll pass on that, but this place is incredible." Her gaze traveled the large greenhouse, maze of heirloom roses, and rustic, Spanish-style structure housing the gift shop. "Why didn't Grant and Eliza consider getting married here?"

"After all they've been through, it's important to them to get married in their hometown."

"That makes sense," she said softly, an unreadable expression clouding her features.

Reed longed to know what she was thinking. "Did you ever consider getting married back home?"

"Not really. For one, home is a complicated term for me. And

Steven wanted to get married in New York, where he was born and raised. He had stronger ties than I did, so I didn't mind. Besides, he said our wedding would be a calling card for my event-planning business."

"That's pretty savvy," he said, trying to be generous. In reality, he thought it sounded way too calculating and not at all romantic.

"Actually, Reed"—she gazed up at him, her countenance earnest yet vulnerable—"there's something—"

"Reed! Over here!" His friend and tour guide for the day, Isabella Russo, beckoned to them through the crowd, headed in their direction.

"I'm sorry." Feeling torn, he offered, "I can tell her we need a few minutes."

"No, that's okay," she said quickly. "It can wait."

"You sure?"

When she nodded, he regretfully wrenched his gaze from her forced smile to return Isabella's wave, making a mental note to reopen the conversation later.

But he didn't want to wait too long.

Whatever she had to say seemed important.

CHAPTER TEN

*S*quelching her confession for a better time, Olivia watched the woman weave through the throng toward them.

She'd been trying to find the right moment to confide in Reed, but something kept getting in the way. And the longer she waited, the more it weighed on her heart. Unfortunately, for the next few hours they'd be on a tour of the nursery, and her thoughts would be focused on selecting the additional flowers they needed for the wedding.

"It's so nice to see you." The dark-haired beauty in a sapphire-hued velvet gown leaned in for a hug, which Reed willingly reciprocated.

Olivia observed the exchange with uneasy interest. They seemed like good friends, close in age with a mutual interest in horticulture. And although she wasn't proud of the thought, she wondered if they'd ever dated. At a cursory glance, they made an ideal couple. Even more so than Reed and Lucy, who couldn't be more opposite.

"Thanks for letting us intrude on a private event." Reed

flashed an appreciative smile. "We're in crunch mode if we have any hope of getting the venue ready in time."

"It's my pleasure," the woman said sincerely, before her full lips arched into a teasing grin. "Plus, I couldn't miss the opportunity to see you in a ruffled blouse."

Olivia stifled an unexpected laugh as Reed pretended to be offended.

"I beg your pardon. But I thought I looked rather dashing in this blouse."

"Oh, you certainly do. You two make the best-looking Romeo and Juliet I've ever seen."

Caught off guard, Olivia blushed at the woman's compliment, stealing a glance at Reed.

He looked momentarily flustered before quickly recovering and making their introduction. "Isabella, this is my friend, Olivia. Olivia, this is Isabella."

"It's so nice to meet you." Isabella shook her hand with surprising warmth. "Reed couldn't stop bragging about how you're a big-time event planner in New York. He's incredibly proud. And rightfully, so. Your résumé is quite exceptional."

Olivia's blush deepened as Reed cleared his throat, clearly not expecting his friend to sell him out.

"That's kind of you to say," Olivia told her, trying not to over-analyze Reed's praise. "But I think what you've done here is phenomenal. The way you've seamlessly transformed an operational nursery into an event venue is brilliant. And this wedding…" She gestured toward the flurry of festive merriment unfolding before them. "I'm impressed by the attention to detail."

And, if she were honest with herself, a tad envious. She would've loved to own an event space.

That is, before she'd lost everything.

"Thank you." Isabella beamed, surveying her work with a glimmer of pride in her dark eyes. "You should have heard me on the phone trying to order an archery set for a wedding. The poor clerk sounded so confused."

"Archery?" Olivia scanned the revelry, searching for signs of bow-and-arrow-wielding wedding guests.

"Don't worry." Isabella offered a reassuring smile, noting her wary expression. "We set it up in between the rows of sunflowers on the other side of the greenhouse. It'll give guests something to do if they don't know the volta."

Based on their blank stares, she explained, "It's a Renaissance-style dance. Believe me, before planning this wedding, I didn't know what it was, either."

"Sounds like you have a lot going on," Reed said with a twinge of guilt. "I know my way around if you want to forgo the tour. We can make a list of flowers we need and drop it off before we leave."

Isabella narrowed her eyes with a playful glint. "You're not trying to sneak into Father's greenhouse, are you?"

"I wouldn't dare!" Reed threw up his hands in a show of innocence. "Besides, I doubt we'd make it past the armed guards even if we tried."

"That's true," Isabella laughed before turning to Olivia. "Primrose Valley holds an annual rose festival. And part of the celebration is a competition for the most exquisite and unusual rose. My father's won... how many times, is it?" she asked Reed with a teasing grin.

"Too many to count. But this year, I have him beat."

"You wish!"

As Olivia watched them banter back and forth, she realized how much she'd missed while living in New York. She'd never even heard of the festival, let alone had any idea Reed would be competing. Why hadn't he mentioned it? If she was still in town, she'd love to show her support.

"I suppose I'll trust that you're not here to spy on Father's winning rose, and let Monte show you around," Isabella relented.

"I vow on the *Farmers' Almanac* that we won't go anywhere near the greenhouse." Reed raised his right hand as though making a legally binding oath.

As they said goodbye for the time being and headed away from the crowd to meet up with Monte, Olivia's spirits fell.

Now that she'd decided to tell Reed the truth, she wondered if they'd ever get a minute alone.

*T*ruthfully, Reed was glad Isabella wouldn't be joining them.

He hoped that touring the nursery by themselves would provide an opportunity to revisit their earlier conversation. Whatever Olivia had been about to say sounded pressing.

As they neared a modest stable, a shaggy Shetland pony lifted his head from a patch of grass and whinnied in greeting.

"Hey, Monte. Long time no see." Reed ran a hand along the horse's thick, caramel coat.

"This is Monte?" Immediately enamored with the adorable animal, Olivia wasted no time stroking his sandy-colored mane. "He's the cutest thing I've ever seen. Besides Nips, of course."

"I'll be sure to tell him you said so." Reed chuckled, pleased she had such an affinity for his feathered friend. "Isabella's father got Monte to pull the buggy, but he quickly became a beloved family pet."

"You and Isabella seem close," she said with an inquisitive inflection.

Ill-prepared for this topic of conversation, Reed busied himself with attaching Monte to the tiny two-person buggy while he formulated a response. "We, uh, went on a few dates a while back. But we decided we were better as friends."

An unreadable expression crossed her features, piquing his interest. "What?"

"It's nothing." She gave a small shrug.

"Spill it," he persisted, his curiosity escalating with each passing second.

"I guess I find it interesting that you and Isabella didn't work out. You seem to have so much in common. While you and Lucy are so different."

"What does Lucy have to do with anything?" Straightening, he stared at her in confusion.

"Don't get me wrong, Lucy is great," she said hastily, her cheeks coloring. "And I suppose it's like the old adage goes… opposites attract and all that." Her entire face burned crimson now, and she appeared genuinely uncomfortable, as though she regretted saying anything at all.

"Wait. You think Lucy and I are a couple?"

"Aren't you?"

"Not even close!" Baffled, he ran a hand through his hair, trying to make sense of her assumption. "What made you think that we were?"

"Oh, well… I…" She shuffled her feet in the loose gravel, gazing at the ground as she composed an explanation. Finally, she glanced up with a sheepish smile. "Well, I'm thoroughly embarrassed."

He chuckled at her candor. "How do you think I feel? Apparently, I've had a girlfriend this whole time and didn't even know it."

The tension slipped away as she laughed at his silly joke. "I'm so sorry I assumed you were together. I should have just asked you."

"Don't worry about it." He waved away her apology, although he couldn't help wondering if she'd been even the slightest bit jealous. But then, why would she?

Pushing aside the thought, he gestured toward the buggy. "Hop on."

After settling beside her on the bench seat, he gave the reins a gentle tap, and Monte sprang forward.

They rode in silence for a few minutes, listening to the rhythmic clomp of hooves on the dirt trail and the festive music warbling in the distance. Occasionally, Olivia would point out a particular bloom she wanted for the wedding, then jotted it down in her phone.

As they neared the end of the tour, Reed worried he'd miss his opening and impulsively blurted, "Earlier, you seemed like you were about to tell me something."

"You're right," she admitted, her gaze falling to her lap. "I've been anxious to tell you all day, but now that I have the chance, it's much harder than I thought."

"Liv," he said gently. "You know you can tell me anything, right?"

Although she nodded, her eyes welled with tears.

Overcome with concern, Reed nudged Monte off the path and paused beside a small pond.

Unclipping the harness, he let the horse wander to the water's edge for a cool drink before turning to face her. "Whatever it is, I'm here for you."

"Thanks," she said with a slight tremor.

For several agonizing seconds, she didn't speak as she slowly twisted the diamond ring around her finger. Finally, she gazed up at him, her lavender-hued eyes glistening with a piercing sadness.

Instinctively, he reached for her hand and gave it a squeeze.

"Steven and I are no longer married," she murmured, barely above a whisper.

"What?" He'd heard the words, but they didn't make sense.

"We're... divorced." The ugly syllables escaped her lips in a strangled breath, and her features crumbled. "It was finalized several months ago."

His gut wrenching, he scooted closer on the bench and wrapped his arm around her. "Liv, what happened?"

He couldn't fathom anyone wanting to be apart from her for two minutes, let alone a lifetime.

"It's a tale as old as time, I suppose." She tried to sound light-hearted, but her voice broke.

He leaned in even closer, as though by sheer proximity his body could absorb her pain.

Her shoulders slumped and defeated, she continued to stare into her lap, spinning the ring as tears trailed down her pallid cheeks. As she spoke, her tone carried a palpable mix of shame and heartache. "The story goes something like: Boy meets girl. Boy marries girl. Boy falls out of love with girl. Boy asks girl for a divorce."

His mind reeled, trying to come to terms with what she was telling him, but he couldn't comprehend anyone falling out of love with her.

He'd tried for years and it didn't seem possible.

"Liv, I'm so sorry. I—What can I do?" Distressed beyond words, he fought his instinct to hop on a flight to New York and confront Steven for being a colossal jerk.

"Nothing." She wiped her damp cheeks with the back of her hand. "But please don't tell anyone."

"No one knows?" That would mean she'd carried the secret on her own for almost a year. The realization made his stomach clench.

"Your mom knows. She guessed the night I came over for dinner. She said she could see it in my eyes."

That sounded like his mom. But how had he missed it? Guilt, remorse, and anger at his own inattention grappled inside his head. He should've known. "I'm so sorry I didn't see it."

"Reed, you couldn't have known. My own family hasn't even figured it out. Your mom and I have a special bond. We're in the same club now." She attempted a wry smile, but her heartbreak hung like a veil around her face.

71

And he would do anything to lift it. "I wish there was something I could do."

"Keep my secret. For now. I plan on telling everyone after the wedding. But I don't want to ruin Grant and Eliza's big day."

While he hated the idea of keeping a secret from Grant, he nodded.

"Thank you." She sighed wearily, as though a tremendous weight had been lifted off her shoulders, and she leaned against him. "I'm so glad it's no longer a secret between us."

He rested his head on hers, drawing her closer, but didn't respond.

How could he?

She'd confessed her secret....

But he still had one of his own.

CHAPTER ELEVEN

*A*s Reed trudged up the staircase to his tree house, each step felt weighed down.

No matter how hard he tried to wrap his head around it, he still couldn't believe Steven had asked for a divorce. What could possibly possess a person to walk out on a woman like Olivia? Didn't Steven realize he'd never find anyone who could even remotely compare?

He should know. He'd been trying for years.

Nips's cheerful greeting did little to assuage his troubled thoughts, and as he prepared dinner, he went through the motions on autopilot.

Dwelling on Olivia's confession dredged up memories he preferred to keep buried. But despite his best efforts, his mind kept wandering to the day he found out about his parents' divorce.

He'd been strolling up the lane on his way home for lunch and spotted a familiar yellow convertible in the driveway, the top down. Candice Conway, the young and ambitious attorney handling the sale of his father's sports memorabilia business, sat in the driver's seat, applying her lipstick in the rearview mirror.

As Reed pushed open the garden gate, he saw his father emerge through the front door, his countenance drawn and ashen.

Upon seeing Reed, Bruce opened his mouth to speak, but the words seemed to catch in his throat. A brief flicker of anguish and remorse distorted his father's features before he pressed his lips into a thin line of resignation.

Without a word, he strode past his son and slid into the passenger seat of Candice's car.

Seconds later, they'd disappeared in a cloud of dust.

His father never looked back.

With a sickening dread in his stomach, Reed entered the house, calling his mother's name.

That's when he'd found her crumpled in a corner of the couch, sobbing into her hands.

His heart had shattered in that moment. As had his world.

In all his life, he'd never felt so powerless—like a young boy again, inept and outside his depth. He'd so badly wanted to take her pain away, but didn't know how. And when he thought of Olivia suffering the same soul-wrenching grief as his mother, the familiar helplessness returned tenfold.

But while he may not be able to do anything about her broken marriage, perhaps he could do something to help soothe her broken heart.

As an idea gripped him, he pulled out his phone and texted her to meet him by the creek after dark.

Abandoning his dinner on the kitchen counter, he set about his plan.

ith both hands covering her eyes, Olivia stumbled over an uneven patch of dirt.

Quick to steady her, Reed slipped his hand around her waist, resting it on the small of her back. "We're almost there."

"Where are we going? And why do I have to cover my eyes? It's pitch-black out."

"You'll see," he said cryptically.

She heard the smile in his voice and her heart beat a bit faster.

In light of her mortifying confession earlier that afternoon, she'd almost declined his invitation tonight, preferring to stay home and wallow. But she had a feeling from the way he'd worded his text that he wouldn't take no for an answer.

They walked in silence for a few more minutes, the only sounds the melodic crickets and crunching of twigs beneath their feet.

All the while, Reed kept a guiding hand on her back, and she savored the warmth of his touch through her thin sweater.

Finally they paused, and Reed removed his palm, taking the warmth with him. "Okay, you can look now."

She slowly lowered her hands and opened her eyes, gasping in surprise.

Their old tree house shone beneath the glimmer of twinkling string lights. And a thick pile of blankets and pillows formed a cozy lounge area. "What's all this?"

"Come up and find out." He led the way up the rope ladder, helping her climb onto the platform.

That's when she noticed the basket filled with her favorite childhood snack—Reese's Peanut Butter Cups. Plus, she recognized a pastry box with the logo of The Calendar Café, and her mouth watered just thinking about what delicious desserts might be inside.

"This is amazing. But I don't understand. What's all of this for?"

"What's a movie night without junk food?" He grinned, nodding over his shoulder.

She followed his gaze toward a white sheet stretched between the branches, pulled taut on all four corners by sturdy rope.

While she gaped in speechless awe, he flipped the switch on a portable projector and the opening credits of the 1960s version of *Swiss Family Robinson* flashed across the makeshift screen.

"You're kidding!" she laughed, overcome with delight. "I haven't seen this movie since we were kids."

"I thought a night of nostalgia might be in order."

Something in the softness of his tone made her throat tighten. He'd gone through all of this trouble just for her. And for the first time in months, she didn't feel alone. "It's perfect. All of it. Thank you, Reed."

Impulsively, she threw her arms around his neck, hugging him tightly as she fought back grateful tears.

"What are friends for?"

Friends.

She hadn't realized how badly she'd needed one until Reed came back into her life. And she would do anything to not lose him again.

Pulling back, she eyed a large cellophane bag of taffy from Sadie's Sweet Shop. "I don't have to share those, do I?"

"No," he chuckled. "But you do have to share the blankets." He plopped onto the makeshift bed and threw back the covers for her to crawl inside. "Remember when we used to camp out under the stars?"

"Of course." She snuggled beside him, leaning against the fluffy mound of pillows. "My face would freeze, but I loved it. The only stars you see in New York are the occasional celebrity sightings."

"Do you miss being in New York?" he asked, passing her the bag of taffy.

"Honestly? Not really. I'd forgotten how much I enjoy the tranquility of the country. Everything is so loud and fast-paced in the city. You can barely hear yourself think."

"What about work? I see the way your face lights up when you're in planning mode."

"I do miss it," she admitted softly. "I took some time off after the divorce, and my assistant filled in for me. It feels good to be planning a wedding again, especially for Grant and Eliza."

"It's great that you had help. I can't imagine going back to work right away after what you'd been through."

She popped a taffy into her mouth to avoid responding, but she barely tasted the sugary confection.

Relying on her assistant had turned out to be a disastrous mistake, in more ways than one. But she didn't want to ruin the perfect evening by dwelling on painful memories from her past.

Right now, she wanted to savor every idyllic detail in the blissful present.

A cool breeze caressed her cheeks and she burrowed deeper into the blankets, relishing the heat from Reed's body nestled against her own.

Curled up beside him, she released a contented sigh.

In that moment, her entire world was at peace.

And she never wanted it to end.

CHAPTER TWELVE

*S*unlight danced across Reed's eyelids, gently rousing him from a deep, gratifying sleep.

The dulcet greeting of robins perched in the overhead branches seemed louder than usual this morning, and his eyes widened as a refreshing puff of cool, crisp air swept across his face.

It took him a moment to register his whereabouts, but the serene, steady breathing by his side gave it away.

He'd fallen asleep in the tree house with Olivia nestled in his arms.

Trying not to wake her with sudden movement, he slowly tilted his chin, taking in the sight of her tousled hair and peaceful, angelic features. Even in sleep, her lips curled into a faint smile.

Although his arm had gone completely numb, he remained motionless, basking in the pure bliss of the moment.

The golden light of morning had given him a gift—a glimpse of what could've been.

When he'd planned the movie night, his only thought had

been to relieve some of the pain she'd been bearing on her own for so long. He'd done it as a friend, nothing more.

But something about the way she curled into him, positioned so perfectly in his arms as if she belonged there, made him question the possibility of more. What if they'd been given a second chance?

A low, velvety moan escaped her lips as she stirred by his side.

Reed held his breath, taking one last mental snapshot of the idyllic scene before it disappeared.

Olivia's smile deepened as her eyelids fluttered open and she glanced up, meeting his gaze. "Good morning."

The smooth purr of her voice sent shivers rippling through him.

"Good morning." His own inflection sounded rough and husky, adding to the intimacy of the exchange.

Could she feel the heat surging between them? Or would she credit the mountain of blankets creating a comfortable cocoon?

Either way, he didn't dare move, waiting for her to react first. He half expected her to scoot away, but she held his gaze, her lavender-hued eyes soft and dreamy.

What was happening? He didn't dare breathe. Or even hope.

She tipped her chin toward him, but in the span of a single second, the sublime bubble burst.

Olivia bolted upright, shock scrawled across her face. "Morning?" As the hour of the day registered, she threw back the covers and scrambled to her feet. "I can't believe we fell asleep. What are my parents going to think?" She dragged her fingers through her tangled hair in a frantic attempt to hide the signs of her wrongdoing, as though she were still a child about to get caught.

"I'm sure once you explain what happened, they'll understand," Reed offered calmly.

She stared at him as though he knew nothing of the world. "I'm a married woman, Reed. Who spent the night alone with another man. Can you even fathom the impropriety?" She straightened her sweater with a few agitated tugs before turning toward the ladder.

As he watched her scurry to the ground, he thought better of reminding her that she wasn't technically married anymore.

What would be the point? According to everyone else in town, she was still Mrs. Steven Rockford III.

Which meant whatever was or wasn't happening between them didn't matter.

*A*s Olivia crept inside, her muscles tensed, waiting for her parents to greet her with frowns of disapproval, followed by a stinging reprimand.

But the entire house sat still and silent, without so much as the gentle gurgle of the coffee maker.

With a heavy sigh of relief, she quietly tiptoed upstairs, heading straight for the shower.

Hopefully, the hot water would help clear her addled thoughts.

For the briefest moment that morning, somewhere between deep sleep and full consciousness, she'd woken up next to Reed and experienced complete contentment, as if her heart knew something her mind refused to acknowledge.

But even considering the possibility of pursuing more than friendship made her stomach clench in anxious knots. Reed had been there for her when she needed him most. What would happen if they tried crossing the line? She couldn't bear losing him again.

And clearly, her track record of romantic relationships wasn't the greatest.

After her shower, she decided to dedicate herself to wedding planning, giving her mind—and heart—a much-needed break. Even though Grant and Eliza had already settled many of the details, the change in venue would require significant alterations. And after months of planning, they were both grateful to entrust the remaining tasks to her capable hands.

Lost in the realm of dance floor rentals and confirming caterers, Olivia finally relaxed. She may not be able to control her own life, but she could plan an event better than anyone else she knew.

And that included Emily Cargill—aka the worst assistant in the world.

Humiliation still washed over her every time she thought about how she'd once considered Emily a good friend. They used to go everywhere together, even when they weren't working— yoga, wine tasting, off-Broadway shows. As a striking platinum blond and raven-haired duo, they often drew attention, even winding up in the society columns. Steven used to joke that they were becoming as famous as New York's iconic black-and-white cookies. A comparison she now found unpalatable for more reasons than one.

Shoving aside her laptop, Olivia headed downstairs for a fresh cup of coffee, needing to recenter. She hated when she let her mind wander too far down treacherous roads.

As she entered the kitchen, her mother glanced up from packing a picnic basket. "Hi, sweetheart. Did you sleep well last night?"

"I slept fine," she said in the understatement of the century. Her pulse quickening, she busied herself with preparing the coffeepot. Although she noticed a peculiar intonation in her mother's question, she wouldn't crack under the pressure and reveal last night's blunder unnecessarily.

"Olivia, can I ask you something?"

Uh-oh. Here it comes....

Squaring her shoulders, Olivia turned, bracing herself for the worst.

But her mother didn't look angry or even displeased. Instead, a shadow of concern darkened her elegant features.

"Is everything all right with you and Steven? You've barely mentioned him since you got home."

Olivia sucked in a breath. This was it—the defining moment.

Withholding information was bad enough. But outright lying? That felt so much worse.

But what could she do?

Parting her lips, she prayed her subconscious would summon the right words.

Just then, the doorbell chimed, coming to her rescue.

"I'll get it." Grateful for an escape, she rushed to answer the door, surprised to find Lucy Gardener on the other side.

"Hi!" Lucy smiled brightly. "I'm here to steal you for the Secret Picnic."

"The what?" Olivia blinked in confusion, still unsettled to find the stylish blond standing on her front stoop.

"The Secret Picnic. You know, everyone meets in the town square with a picnic lunch, places all the baskets into a random pile, then picks a different basket than the one they brought before heading to Larkspur Meadow to eat, followed by lawn games." Lucy rattled off the details as though they should jog her memory any second.

"Right." While she vaguely recalled her mother mentioning something about it, Olivia didn't plan on attending. "That's so kind of you, but I really have a lot of wedding stuff to do still…."

"Everyone needs a break once in a while," Lucy quipped, undeterred. "And we won't take no for an answer."

"We?"

"Me, Sadie, and Reed. Sorry, but you're stuck with the singles crowd. Hope you don't mind." She grinned, then added, "We'll all sit together anyway, so the groups are really more of a formality. Luke, Cassie, Grant, and Eliza are going together. Ben's attending with friends. Then there's Jack, Kat, Colt, and Penny in the other foursome."

As Lucy listed off all the names, Olivia's chest tightened. That sounded like an awful lot of people. Too many, to be precise.

Plus, she wanted more time to sort out her confusing emotions before seeing Reed again.

"Um..." She glanced over her shoulder, trying to send a nonverbal SOS to her mother. When she didn't oblige, Olivia said a little too casually, "Mom, weren't you hoping I'd go with you and Dad to the picnic?" At least if she went with her parents she could keep her distance.

"Don't worry about us." Harriet waved away her attempt at deliverance. "Go with your friends and have a good time."

Stifling a groan, Olivia turned back to Lucy, who beamed in delight. "Great! It's settled. Sadie packed our picnic basket, so unless you want to change your shoes or something, we can get going."

Olivia glanced down at her jeans, tank top, and flimsy sandals. While she didn't plan on participating in any of the games, sneakers would be a better choice for the walk from the town square to the meadow.

She plucked them off of the shoe rack by the front door on her way out, suppressing the urge to run upstairs and lock the door behind her.

Although tempting, she reminded herself that she wasn't a petrified little girl anymore.

She could get through one afternoon unscathed... couldn't she?

CHAPTER THIRTEEN

$\mathcal{S}$itting cross-legged on a plaid picnic blanket, Olivia listened to the chatter around her while she nibbled on a grilled artichoke panini. Maybe it was the chipotle lime aioli slathered on the fresh focaccia bread or the scrumptious sriracha sweet potato fries, but she was actually having a good time.

Picnic-goers who'd finished eating now played lawn games, challenging each other to cornhole, bocce ball, and life-size Jenga. The pleasant spring air echoed with gleeful laughter and squeals of merriment, culminating in an infectious energy that could chip through the exterior of even the most hardened cynic.

Despite Olivia's misgivings about the outing, all the women had been warm and inviting, effortlessly including her in the conversation. Since Cassie and Kat were newcomers to Poppy Creek, she wasn't as much of an outsider as she'd feared.

But the observation that weighed on her heart the most had to do with Reed and her brother, Grant. They'd clearly made this eclectic group their second family, trusting them with the most important aspects of their lives. Perhaps their unwavering faith should be reason enough to lower her walls? Or at the very least, lessen some of her inhibitions in the here and now.

While her insecurities still simmered beneath the surface, her anxiety slipped into the background, allowing her to relax and enjoy the moment.

The only downside of the afternoon? Sitting way too close to Reed—a hazard of cramming so many people onto one blanket, even though most of the couples sat in intimate poses with their limbs entangled, some practically sitting in their partner's lap.

Every time her knee grazed Reed's, tingles skittered up her leg, as if taunting her earlier decision to keep things platonic. But why now? She'd finally started to heal. She didn't need this new, unsettling awareness to complicate her already fragile state of mind.

"Who's ready for the three-legged race?" Lucy sprang to her feet, tearing Olivia from her thoughts.

"You all might as well sit this one out, since you don't stand a chance," Colt teased.

"Please." Jack snorted. "You always start off too strong and wind up face-planting before the halfway mark."

"Eliza and Grant are the real threat," Cassie countered with a good-natured smile. "They're dance partners, which gives them a leg up."

"No pun intended," Luke added on behalf of his wife.

Plenty of groans and chuckles followed.

"Sadie and I are about the same height," Lucy pointed out. "So, I think that gives us the advantage."

"Don't forget the summer Reed spent on crutches when he fell out of his tree house," Eliza reminded them. "He's used to hobbling around."

"You fell out of the tree house?" Olivia asked, suddenly concerned.

"I took a tumble off the platform during construction and wound up with a bad sprain. But it healed good as new." Reed untangled his legs and hopped to his feet, as if to prove his point.

For a split second, Olivia wished he could stay and watch the race with her. But her wiser self knew she could use a break from his perplexing presence. The constant ebb and flow of her emotions was enough to make her seasick on solid ground.

But as everyone began pairing off, a disconcerting realization gripped her.

Without her, they had an uneven number.

*H*is heart thundering inside his chest, Reed remained perfectly still while Bill Tucker used duct tape to secure his leg to Olivia's.

She stood so close, he could smell her floral shampoo, and every time a breeze blew by, a few silky strands fluttered against his stubbled cheek.

"Can you scoot closer together?" Bill asked, oblivious to Reed's predicament. "I need to get the tape a smidgen tighter."

Swallowing the lump in his throat, Reed obliged, but he wasn't sure where to rest his hands, so he held them awkwardly at his sides.

Every second that lapsed, his body temperature rose several degrees. And as they stood squished together, he thought for sure she'd notice.

In fact, she looked a tad flushed herself, and kept her gaze glued to Bill's pet pig, Peggy Sue, as she rooted around the picnic blankets for abandoned leftovers.

"There ya go." Bill smiled as he surveyed his handiwork, appearing pleased with the result. "Good luck, you two."

As Bill sauntered off to wrangle the next pair of contestants, Reed glanced down at Olivia. "Can you still feel the circulation in your leg?"

"Barely." She laughed, then wobbled.

He swiftly slipped his arm around her waist, steadying her against his side. The increased physical contact made his pulse

THE FAITH IN FLOWERS

pound in his eardrums and he tried to ignore the way his stomach swirled.

Get it together.

"Do you think we stand a chance?" she asked, adding to his affliction by hitching her thumb in his belt loop to help keep her balance.

He prayed no one noticed that he was slowly falling apart. Any second now, he'd probably become a puddle at her feet.

"You mean against them?" He followed her gaze to where Jack and Colt playfully bantered about who would be eating whose dust.

"Yes. They seem awfully confident, don't they?"

"They always do." He grinned, adding, "But we have something they don't."

"What's that?"

"History."

Her brow wrinkled in confusion. "What do you mean?"

"Jack and Kat just met in December," he explained. "And Colt and Penny didn't even like each other until last summer. But we've been friends for years, which means we have the upper hand."

"Huh. You think so?"

"I know so. Just watch. Once we start running, it'll be like we only have one leg."

She arched an eyebrow.

"Or two legs," he corrected, momentarily confused. "*Two* of our legs will become like one leg. Which, I suppose, means we'll have a total of three.... You know what I mean." Flustered, he clamped his mouth shut. Why did she make him so tongue-tied all of a sudden?

Her lips twitched as though hiding a smile.

To his relief, his phone buzzed in his back pocket, providing a distraction.

RACHAEL BLOOME

Since Olivia's hand was closer, she slipped his phone from its resting place, causing his pulse to spike with the intimate gesture.

As she passed it to him, he concentrated on taking deep breaths to steady his racing heartbeat. But it stopped altogether when he noticed the caller ID flashing across the screen.

Dad.

"You can answer, if you want," Olivia offered kindly.

"Thanks, but that's okay." Without hesitation, he sent the call to voice mail before stuffing his phone back inside his pocket.

"Is it still difficult after the divorce?" Her hushed voice resonated with sympathy.

"We've been trying to patch things up the past year. But it's tough when every time we talk, I can't stop thinking about what he did."

She nodded, her eyes full of understanding.

"What about you? Do you still talk to Steven?" Even as he asked the question, he wasn't sure how he felt about the possibility.

"We haven't spoken since Christmas," she admitted with a pained expression.

He'd often wondered what had happened that day. He keenly remembered her family's concern over their failed attempts to reach her. Worried, he'd placed his own call, hoping he'd have better luck, even though the odds weren't in his favor.

Not surprisingly, she didn't answer.

The next day, he'd asked Grant if they'd ever heard back from her. Apparently, she'd called the morning after Christmas with some flimsy excuse about Steven surprising her and not being able to talk on the phone.

Then, the other night in his tree house, she'd apologized for ignoring his call, but hadn't explained.

Maybe he'd finally find out what had really transpired that day.

"Liv, what happened on Christmas? It's still somewhat of a mystery to me."

Her gaze fell to the ground, and for a moment, even though they were side by side, she felt extremely far away.

Before she could respond, a sharp whistle pierced the air, and Mayor Burns called everyone to the starting line.

Reed suppressed a disappointed groan at the mayor's terrible timing.

Over the last several days, Olivia had divulged a lot, especially considering her more reserved nature. While he wanted to be there for her, he didn't want to push. She would tell him when she was ready.

For now, he'd have to be patient.

CHAPTER FOURTEEN

*C*lutching her second-place ribbon, Olivia climbed into the passenger seat of Lucy's car with an uncontrollable grin.

She couldn't remember the last time she'd had so much fun, and she was grateful to Lucy for talking her into coming.

While she and Reed had lost to a pair of scrappy high schoolers, he'd been right about how well they worked together.

"I had a blast today," Lucy gushed as she backed out of her parking spot. "I'd forgotten how much I missed this place."

"I thought you grew up here."

"I did. Until high school. Then my family moved to Primrose Valley. I love it there, too. But this town will always feel like home."

Olivia let this news settle in, realizing she knew very little about Lucy. To her surprise, she found herself interested in getting to know her better.

"What about you?" Lucy asked.

"Honestly? I'm not sure," Olivia admitted. "There was a time when I considered Poppy Creek home. And I was pretty devastated when my parents made me leave."

Her heart still ached when she recalled the night she'd overheard her parents discussing her future. They were concerned with how withdrawn she'd become and her mother mentioned a boarding school her friend, Mitsy Davenport, swore by.

At first, her father had been outraged by the suggestion. He'd moved them to Poppy Creek with the sole purpose of saving her from the cruelty she'd suffered at her previous school in New York.

But Harriet had insisted that she had a plan this time. Mitsy's daughter, Pricilla, had agreed to take Olivia under her wing.

While Olivia couldn't help feeling like a pity project, she'd never forget the haunting sound of her mother's sobs as she begged her father to consider the proposition as a last resort to undo the debilitating damage and "fix" her.

In the end, the plan had worked. She'd finally made her mother proud. And if Harriet ever found out how low she'd sunk, she'd be devastated.

"I'm so sorry," Lucy said sincerely. "I had no idea. I always thought you'd wanted to go. To be honest, at that age, I was a bit jealous. It all sounded so glamorous."

Olivia smiled wistfully. Lucy would've been a natural, if they'd traded places. It had taken her much longer to fit in. And now, she wasn't sure if she ever had.

"It had some good moments, too." A vivid memory of the first time she met Steven flashed into her mind, but she quickly pushed it aside, focusing on the picturesque meadows zipping by as Lucy maneuvered the winding mountain roads in her Mercedes.

"I'm sure it did." Lucy grinned, and Olivia could tell from her inflection that she meant her marriage to Steven. "Can I ask you something kind of personal?" Lucy added with a tentative twinge.

Olivia's heartbeat faltered. Did Lucy suspect something? Had her expression given it away?

Before she could answer, Lucy continued. "I sort of... have my eye on this guy." Her fair complexion flushed slightly, but she pressed on with her question. "I'm wondering how you know when someone has long-term potential? If you haven't noticed, all of our friends are still in the honeymoon stages, and I thought someone who's been married awhile would have more time-tested advice."

Stunned, Olivia sat motionless, unsure how to respond. She certainly wasn't in any position to give that kind of counsel. But what could she say without revealing her secret?

Her thoughts immediately flew to the one person outside of her family who'd proven to be a lasting and loyal fixture in her life, and the words flowed freely. "I think the most important thing to recognize is that outward appearance and external qualities don't matter nearly as much as a person's character." Her heart warmed as she thought of all the ways Reed had earned her trust and admiration over the years. But almost instantly, the fond recollection collided with another reality—the one she relived every time she glanced at her ring.

Twisting the cool metal band, she murmured, "Trust me, integrity lasts a lot longer than infatuation."

Lucy appeared to let her wisdom sink in before bestowing a grateful smile. "Thank you for that. That's exactly what I needed to hear. I knew asking you was the right decision. And I'm really happy you have that kind of man in your life."

"Me, too," Olivia said softly, her thoughts churning.

Impulsively, she reached for her phone and pulled up a familiar number.

Before she could change her mind, she composed the text and pressed Send.

*F*or the second time in the past fifteen minutes, Reed tugged the navy blue polo over his head and reassessed his appearance in the mirror. "What do you think?" He glanced over his shoulder at Nips, who bobbed on the nearby perch. "Yeah, I like this one better, too."

He slid the lime-green polo back on its hanger, his pulse skittering in anticipation.

There'd been something about Olivia's invitation to meet tonight that made him restless and nervous, but also excited.

It wasn't so much what she'd said in her text, but what he could read between the lines. It didn't seem like a regular hang night.

Then again, he could be misreading things and didn't want to get his hopes up too high.

Although, it may already be too late for that.

All afternoon, he'd watched Olivia blossom before his eyes. Her smile had been transcendent.

Growing up, he'd longed for the day when she'd let down her walls. While he loved being best friends, he knew she needed more than he could offer on his own—she needed what he'd already found in his friend group. And his heart broke a little more each time she refused his attempts to include her.

But today, she'd finally allowed herself to open up. And it was the most beautiful thing he'd ever seen. He also knew that whatever she'd gain by allowing these people into her life, she would be an even bigger blessing in return. He only wished she could see that for herself.

His phone buzzed on the nightstand and he glanced at the screen, wondering if she'd arrived early. She'd said to meet her at their old tree house and offered to bring something for dinner.

When he saw that it was his father calling yet again, Reed groaned. Leave it to his dad to ruin his good spirits.

RACHAEL BLOOME

It buzzed again, signaling another voice mail. That would be the third one today.

Somewhat reluctantly, he pressed Play.

"Hey, son. I know things are complicated between us right now, but I really need you to do something for me. For your mother, actually. It's our thirty-third anniversary today."

Immediately, panic rose in Reed's throat. His heart pounded as his father's strained words pierced through the speaker.

"I forgot that on a trip a few years ago, I ordered something that's supposed to be delivered today. I need you to intercept the package before she sees it. I don't care what you do with it after that."

Even before the message came to an end, Reed dashed toward the door, propelled by a potent mixture of anger, fear, and guilt.

He prayed he could reach his mother in time.

CHAPTER FIFTEEN

*A*fter trying on various outfits, Olivia settled on her favorite pair of jeans and a lavender cardigan, aware of how it intensified the violet hue of her eyes.

As she studied her features in the mirror, she thought of all the times Steven had praised her physical appearance. They were always vague flatteries like *You're the most beautiful woman in the room* and *You're a first-place trophy wife.*

While Reed didn't pay her those kinds of compliments, a seemingly offhand comment several years ago had meant far more to her than he could have realized.

They'd been discussing attempts by a Japanese company to produce the world's first blue rose, speculating on what particular shade of blue they hoped to achieve.

Reed mentioned that if he were in charge of the project, he'd make the rose the same color as her eyes. For weeks afterward, she couldn't glance at her reflection without smiling.

Even now, she cherished his words. And the soft look of admiration he'd given her as he said them.

Speaking with Lucy on the way home from the picnic had made her realize how lucky she was to have a man like Reed in her life. And maybe it was worth seeing if there could be something more between them.

She hoped to find out tonight.

The sound of her mother calling her name from the bottom of the staircase yanked Olivia from her thoughts.

"Coming," she shouted before applying one last layer of nude lipstick.

She found her mother in the living room, holding a large portrait over the mantel. "Can you tell me if this is straight?"

Olivia's blood ran cold as her gaze landed on the smiling couple in the gilded frame. "M-Mom, what are you doing?"

Harriet lowered the photograph and leaned it against the hearth before turning to face her. "With your brother's wedding around the corner, I thought it would be nice to do some redecorating. I'm going to hang your wedding photo here and that empty frame is for Grant and Eliza's. Your father and I will be in the middle. Don't you think it'll look nice?"

Olivia opened her mouth to respond, but her throat constricted around her words.

She and Steven looked so happy, so hopelessly in love. Even the way they leaned into each other, as though they'd never be close enough, gave the impression of a couple destined for happily ever after.

How had things gone so terribly wrong?

Sure, she'd had her doubts about their relationship in the beginning. There were even times early on when she'd wondered what life would be like if she'd never left Poppy Creek—if she'd never left Reed.

But she'd loved Steven, even though their marriage had been far from perfect. And she'd thought he'd loved her.

In the end, their fairy tale had become a nightmare. And they'd gone the way of so many marriages before them.

"It'll look great," she lied, her voice hoarse.

Her mother smiled, although she didn't seem completely

convinced. "You look nice, sweetheart. Are you going somewhere?"

Olivia hesitated.

Faced with the taunting image of her tragic failure, her resolve unraveled.

As did her plans for the evening.

*W*ithout stopping to catch his breath, Reed sprinted through the garden gate.

If only he hadn't avoided his father's phone calls all afternoon. What if he arrived too late?

He'd never forgive himself if he didn't intercept the package in time.

He also wouldn't forgive his father for putting them all in this position in the first place. But Bruce Hollis had made a habit of putting his own feelings before everyone else's.

Racing up the pathway, he searched for any sign of a special delivery, but no packages were in sight. He even checked behind the large terra-cotta pot housing the monstrous sunburst succulent and the kitschy bench made out of recycled shipping pallets.

But he found nothing.

His spirits sank. He was too late.

His only hope was that she'd brought the package inside but hadn't opened it yet.

Without knocking, he pushed through the front door. "Mom?"

No answer.

He frantically checked each room, ending in the kitchen.

His mother sat at the dining table, a cardboard box and packing material littered around her like shrapnel.

Tears stained her cheeks and she didn't look up when he

entered, her watery gaze fixed on a small object clutched in her hands.

"Mom." He spoke softer now, sitting beside her as his chest tightened. "Are you okay?"

"It's our thirty-third anniversary today." Her voice sounded hollow with grief.

"I know. Dad called. He wanted me to find this before you did." Reed reached for whatever lay hidden in her grasp, but she tightened her hold.

"I assumed he'd forgotten he sent it. The card said, *Faithfully yours*." She attempted a wry smile, but a strangled sob escaped.

"Mom, let me take that." He leaned forward, desperate to remove the item causing her so much pain, but she wouldn't release it.

Instead, she held it up for him to see. "It's a carnation coral encased in resin," she explained, sniffling as she tried not to cry. "We stumbled upon this little shop on our thirtieth anniversary trip to the coast. I fell in love with it and your father wanted to buy it for me. I told him to surprise me on our thirty-third, since coral is the traditional gift. I never thought he'd actually do it. But he must've placed the order that same day to ship at a later date."

Seething with anger, Reed noted how fitting the gift had turned out to be, since the yellow carnation represented disappointment and rejection.

"I'm so sorry, Mom." Seeing her so distraught made his chest ache. He wanted to take the trinket and smash it into a thousand minuscule pieces. But she still wouldn't let go.

"I'm actually glad I found it."

"Why?" He didn't see how her finding it could be anything but a complete disaster—a disaster he could have prevented.

"Since the day your father left, I've been tormented over how long he'd been wanting to leave me. Had he been unhappy for decades and I just never saw it? But this..." She traced her fingertip along the smooth surface. "This means that three years ago today, less than a year before he left, he was planning on being around for our thirty-third anniversary."

Hearing the quiet hopefulness in her voice took him by surprise. After all these years, and everything he'd done, she still loved his father. It didn't make sense.

"Mom," he said gently, tiptoeing toward his question. "Was it worth it?"

"Marrying your father?"

Nodding, he added, "And not just because of me and Mark. Would you choose to love Dad if you could go back and do it all over again?"

He expected her to take a moment to ponder his question, but she replied without hesitation. "Yes, it was worth it. Love is always a risk. I still pray for him every day."

Reed marveled at her steady sincerity and tender resolve. When she'd said her vows thirty-three years ago, she'd meant them—for better or for worse. And he realized, if Olivia were his wife, there wasn't a single mountain he wouldn't climb to bridge a gap between them.

He leaned forward and pressed a kiss to her temple. "I'm going to make us some tea."

While he waited for the water to boil, he composed a text to Olivia, explaining that his mother needed him, without going into too many details. Knowing she'd understand, he asked if they could reschedule for the following evening.

She immediately texted back, telling him not to worry. And true to her caring nature, added that if there was anything she could do to help, to please let him know.

His heart warmed at her response, further solidifying his desire to pursue her with every fiber in his being.

And no matter how much time she needed to heal, she was well worth the wait.

CHAPTER SIXTEEN

*A*fter rescheduling her plans with Reed, Olivia spent the evening and following morning wrestling with her afflicted thoughts.

No matter how much progress she made, the smallest reminder of her failed marriage sent her stumbling back several steps, trapped in an endless cycle of shame and regret. She desperately wanted to escape and move forward with her life, but she didn't know how.

She feared the divorce had broken her beyond repair.

A knock on her bedroom door tore her attention from her laptop screen, which she'd been staring at blankly for the last half hour.

Grant stuck his head inside. "Busy?"

"A little," she admitted, not really in the mood for company.

"Too busy for your nephew?" Grinning, he layered on the guilt. "We're going fishing with Dad at the lake, and Ben really wants you to come."

She wavered. "You know I can't resist Ben."

"Yep. I was counting on it." Grant chuckled as he waited for her to put her laptop away and slip on her sandals, as though worried she'd change her mind.

But it turned out, the drive to Willow Lake was exactly what Olivia needed to clear her head. The weather couldn't have been more glorious, and she'd forgotten how beautiful it was with the snowcapped mountains in the distance and shady pine trees dotting the shoreline.

Grant and Olivia settled in camping chairs with thermoses of piping-hot coffee while Stan took Ben to the water's edge for fishing lessons. The entire scene unfolded like a touching Father's Day card.

"You and Dad seem to be getting along well," Olivia noted as Stan periodically shot Grant a look of grandfatherly pride over Ben's casting technique.

Grant's features softened. "Yeah, it's hard to believe sometimes. A year ago, I never would have thought it possible. But with Ben in my life, I have a better understanding of some of the tough choices Dad had to make when we were kids."

"I'm really happy for you two," she said with a slight catch in her throat. It had always saddened her that they'd grown so far apart, Grant becoming more and more bitter at their father's workaholic nature, until they barely spoke at all.

Although, in reality, no one in her family was particularly close—an example set by their parents when they were young— which had made it easier to keep her divorce a secret the last several months... until now.

As they watched Stan help Ben adjust the line, Grant stole a sideways glance in her direction. "Dad finally told me why he moved us to Poppy Creek, about the bullying you went through. Why didn't you ever tell me about it?"

She shrugged, suddenly uncomfortable now that she'd become the topic of conversation. "We didn't talk much back then. And besides, it wasn't like you could have done anything about it. We went to different schools."

"I still wish I'd known. You're my kid sister. I feel terrible that I didn't notice what you were going through."

Her heart warmed at the sincerity in his voice. "You were a teenage boy, Grant. I don't blame you for not noticing. Although, you did become a lot more sensitive and observant when you started dating Eliza."

His eyes brightened. "She's the greatest, isn't she? As sappy as it sounds, she really does make me a better person."

"You seem so much happier now that you're back together," Olivia told him, thrilled to witness the change in her brother over the past year. "Honesty, I'm a little surprised you two didn't tie the knot as soon as possible in some quick, simple ceremony."

Grant grinned. "Quick and simple isn't really Eliza's style. Besides, she wanted to take things slow for Ben's sake. He'd been through so much change in such a short amount of time. First, his trouble at school, then finding out he needed glasses. Plus, there was the whole discovering-he-had-a-dad thing." He flashed an off-kilter smile, playfully making light of the most monumental event in both of their lives. "Then, he moved into a new house, got a dog… the list goes on. Eliza thought a longer adjustment period would be good for him, to sort of ease into it, I guess."

"I suppose that makes sense," Olivia said thoughtfully, though she suspected the wait had been hard on her brother.

"It's difficult to say if it was the right choice," Grant admitted. "But as I'm finding out, that's the tough thing about being a parent. Most of your decisions are an educated guess, not from some foolproof playbook."

"Being a parent sounds terrifying."

"Tell me about it." He chucked, then added, "But it's also the greatest thing in the world. Do you and Steven want kids?"

"No," she said abruptly, recalling the countless times since her divorce she'd been grateful they hadn't dragged a child through the pain and heartbreak.

Grant seemed to notice her sudden shift in demeanor and asked, "Is everything okay between you two? You don't talk about him much."

Olivia stiffened, chiding herself for being so emotionally transparent. What could she say? She couldn't lie. But she wasn't ready for the truth....

"Dad! Aunt Liv! I caught one! I caught one!"

Excited, Ben waved them over, and Olivia released a pent-up breath.

How much longer could she keep her secret? The more time passed, the more it ate away at her, leaving her insides numb and hollow.

She hadn't even told Reed the full extent of what happened.

Tonight, that would have to change.

*L*owering the lighter into the clear mason jar, Reed lit the ivory votive candle his mother had loaned him.

While Olivia had volunteered to bring dinner, he'd decided to set the ambiance by arranging a cozy table for two on the deck of his tree house. He wanted something intimate, without being overly romantic, per his mother's suggestion.

After spending all day at the Windsor Place, he'd stopped by the cottage on his way home to check on her. Her spirits had improved, bolstered to find out the self-portrait she'd painted on a whim had sold its first day at the gallery in Primrose Valley.

Encouraged by her good mood, he told her about his plans with Olivia that evening and his intentions to pursue her. Although thrilled by his admission, she'd given him advice he'd taken to heart. She said when it came to pursuing Olivia, timing would be everything. Like transplanting a delicate shrub, moving too early or too late could have a detrimental effect.

Knowing Olivia still had a lot to work through, he'd focus on being a friend and a listening ear, for the time being—something he had a feeling she needed now more than ever.

"Wow, what's all this?" With a take-out bag in hand, Olivia surveyed the setting with an air of subtle admiration. Her gaze traveled from the amber glow of the bistro lights to the flickering candle on the tabletop. Nearby, golden embers glowed in a small firepit, easing the evening chill.

He hoped he hadn't gone overboard. At the last minute, he'd decided against the vase of snapdragons, which would've made it look too much like a date.

"I'm beginning to think I should've opted for something a little fancier than Jack's Diner," she teased, handing him the brown paper bag.

The sweet, tangy scent of Jack's signature barbecue sauce wafted through the opening, making his mouth water. "Tri-tip sandwiches?"

"Yep. And his Garlic Gold Rush Fries."

"Perfect." He arranged everything on the plates he'd prepared while she took a seat at the table. "I hope you still like sarsaparilla." He popped the caps off two ice-cold bottles, setting one in front of her.

"I do!" Her face brightened. "I could never find these in New York. Good tri-tip is hard to find, too. Did you know it's mostly a California thing?"

"That's a shame." As he lowered himself on the chair opposite her, Nips squawked from his perch by the window.

Olivia laughed. "Is he feeling left out?"

"He thinks I'm forgetting something." Reed strode to the windowsill where he'd set a Tupperware container and lifted the lid. "I told you this was for dessert, but if it'll keep you quiet, you can ruin your dinner this once." He offered him the slice of kiwi.

"Won't he fly away with the window open?" Olivia asked.

"I trained him a while ago not to fly too far off. Plus, he knows he's spoiled here." Reed chuckled as Nips gleefully gobbled down his treat. "One more slice." He placed the fruit in his tiny beak before heading back to his seat. "I stopped by Mom's today, and she sent over some of her vegan lemon bars."

"With the blueberry glaze?" Olivia asked eagerly.

"Yep. I know she's feeling better when she bakes anything using actual sugar."

Olivia grinned, then immediately sobered. "I'm just happy to hear she's doing okay."

Although she didn't pry, he heard the curiosity in her voice. "It was their thirty-third anniversary yesterday."

She nodded, her eyes filled with understanding. "My anniversary was four months ago."

His jaw clenched. He hated knowing she'd had to go through it alone. "I'm sorry, Liv. That must've been tough."

"It was. As much as I wanted to stay angry, I couldn't help thinking about all the good times we had."

Reed stared at his sandwich growing cold on his plate. While it pained him to hear about her marriage, he reminded himself that he was her friend. And if it helped her to talk about it, he wanted to be here for her.

"Steven could be sweet when he wanted to be," she said softly. "When he proposed on the day of graduation, he got down on one knee with a bouquet of—"

"Red roses," Reed finished, without thinking. His heart stalled when he realized his mistake.

"Yes, but how did you know that?" She narrowed her eyes in confusion, and his throat went dry.

This was not the right moment to confess his secret. Instead, he chose to deflect. "Red roses are the most popular flower used in proposals."

"Right..." she said slowly, returning to her story. "He proposed with two dozen red roses and told me that I was more beautiful than all of them combined."

Blushing, she glanced down at her lap, twisting the ring

around her finger. "I think that's why I overlooked all the warning signs. After years of being beaten-down and ridiculed, he made me feel attractive and desirable, worthy of someone's love."

As she spoke, his heart ached. He wanted to shout that he'd loved her, more than she could ever know. But he remained silent, recognizing her need to be heard and process her thoughts.

"I spent our entire marriage measuring my value against Steven's opinion of me. And I lost so much of myself in the process. But I thought I'd finally become his perfect woman, which is why…" Her voice quivered and when she lifted her chin to meet his gaze, her eyes glistened with unshed tears. "Reed, there's something I need to tell you, but I don't know how. The words feel… stuck."

His own eyes stung with emotion at her vulnerable confession.

Their food forgotten, he stood and held out his hand. "Come with me."

Without hesitation, she slipped her hand in his.

Nimbly, he pulled her to her feet. "I have this place I like to go when my worries feel especially heavy. Somehow, they all seem to fall away."

He hoped it would afford her the same comfort.

CHAPTER SEVENTEEN

*T*ucked against Reed in a nylon hammock suspended several feet above the ground, Olivia had never felt safer despite their seemingly precarious position.

Hidden among the tree branches, her body hovered completely weightless in the still night air, as though every stifling fear and insecurity had floated toward the stars overhead. Each glittering speck in the vast expanse of inky black seemed to put her singular experience in perspective.

"When I told you about the divorce, I left something out," she admitted softly. "Everything happened just like I said… until Christmas morning."

As hurtful memories tumbled to the forefront of her mind, she nestled closer to Reed, comforted by the rhythmic rise and fall of his chest.

"Waking up alone on my first Christmas after the divorce was harder than I'd imagined. Desperate for a distraction, I headed into the office for the first time in months. I knew Emily was working on a New Year's Eve party for a client, and I thought it would help take my mind off things. But when I arrived, I discovered the locks had been changed."

Reed stiffened by her side, as though sensing trouble.

Gathering a breath, she kept her gaze fixed on the myriad of stars, tracing the outline of the Big Dipper to keep herself calm.

"I didn't want to panic right away. There could be several reasonable explanations. I had talked to Emily about making her a partner since she'd been such a huge help. So, I thought maybe she'd decided to have new locks and keys made. Before I disrupted her Christmas over nothing, I went back home and tried to access our shared server on my laptop. But all the passwords had been changed. At that point, I tried calling her, but she didn't answer."

Reed's once-steady breath came in shorter, faster bursts, and she could tell he was trying to remain composed for her sake, but didn't seem happy with the direction her story had taken.

Fighting against her own crumbling emotions, she drew solace from the gentle motion of his fingertips running up and down her arm.

"My last resort was pulling up my list of client contacts. But it had been wiped clean. Every name and number, except for the few I'd saved in my phone, were gone. Fearing the worst, I drove to Emily's apartment."

Tears filled her eyes, smudging the stars into a shimmering blur, and she squeezed them shut.

For a moment, she wanted to retreat, not sure if she could manage another word.

But she'd come this far. And she wanted to get everything out in the open, once and for all.

Taking a deep breath, she exhaled slowly. "Emily answered the door in her pajamas and she looked so surprised, I started to second-guess myself. Maybe there was a reasonable explanation after all. I reminded myself that we'd been friends for years. And she was the only one who hadn't abandoned me after the divorce. Plus, it was Christmas. The conversation could probably wait until the following day. Believing I'd let my insecurities and fears get the best of me, I apologized for barging in on her and turned to go. That's when—" Her voice broke, despite her best efforts to keep it together, and Reed pulled her closer.

As their weight shifted, she slid on the slick nylon fabric, molding to his frame. With her head now resting on his chest, she heard his heart beating, as though assuring her of his unwavering presence.

Bolstered by his nearness, she murmured, "That's when Steven appeared behind her, wearing the same red satin pajamas."

"Liv..." Her name escaped his lips in a pained gasp, and the distress and concern saturating the single syllable instantly soothed her heart.

She wasn't alone anymore.

The truth wrapped around her like a comforting blanket.

"What did you do?" His gruff inflection indicated that he hoped she'd let Steven have it.

"I was so shocked, I didn't even react," she confessed, her cheeks flushed with shame. "I just stood there in the dimly lit hallway as he glossed over the affair, which had apparently been going on for over a year. He went on to explain how he'd talked Emily into taking over the business, and they'd already told all of my clients that I'd resigned and had willingly handed Emily the reins."

"They can't do that," he seethed through gritted teeth.

"They could because Steven knew all of my insecurities." A single tear slipped from the corner of her eye, searing her skin as it slid down her cheek, landing on his soft cotton T-shirt. "He knew that if I had to go up against Emily, I truly believed I'd lose. And seeing them together that morning only confirmed my worst fear—I'd never be good enough."

On a broken sob, she buried her face against his chest, overcome with both relief and regret after bearing her soul.

Suddenly fearful, she prayed her sordid tale wouldn't change his opinion of her.

She couldn't bear his pity or to lose his esteem.

Exposed and vulnerable, she held her breath, waiting in agony for his response.

*B*urning with anger, Reed struggled to breathe.

One hand curved around Olivia's upper arm, the other lay clenched at his side, longing to make contact with Steven's face—both for the affair and for the despicable business move.

How could someone be so vile and malicious?

He felt sick even thinking about it.

But more than that, his heart broke for Olivia; he was completely gutted by how demoralized she'd become by it all.

"You are more than enough," he said with fierce veracity. "You are Olivia Parker, an extraordinary woman who cares deeply and loves with her whole heart. Despite all the pain you've experienced at the hands of others, you're the first person to help someone in need. You're strong yet soft and empathetic. And all those qualities make you the best event planner anywhere, not just in New York." His voice rumbled with a conviction he felt deep in his core, and yet, his description didn't even scratch the surface of her character.

"Watching the way you work with Grant and Eliza, you have this remarkable ability to listen while also anticipating desires they haven't expressed. As an event planner, and a human being, your caliber is unlike any other. Steven and Emily may have stolen your contacts, but they could never steal your business. Because it's nothing without you."

Suddenly winded, he felt his muscles melt into the hammock as the adrenaline drained from his body.

He wanted to say so much more, but needed to collect his thoughts before confessing too much.

This night wasn't about him. He could see now more than ever that Olivia needed more time to discover her worth outside of a man's—*any* man's—estimation. As her friend, his role would be to point her in the right direction.

Olivia lifted her chin, her misty eyes sparkling in the moonlight. "Thank you," she murmured, her voice thick and breathy.

As he held her gaze, an overwhelming longing to press his lips against hers tingled through every nerve ending. And it took everything in his power not to lean down and capture her mouth with his, confirming his resolution would be so much harder than he could fathom.

She needs time, he repeated over and over in his mind, trying to calm his tumultuous heartbeat.

With her hand resting on his chest, he worried she might feel the erratic thrumming beneath her fingertips.

Instinctively, he shifted his weight and she slid even closer, her lips mere inches from his own.

In that moment, the stars overhead seemed to blink into obscurity, and the chirping crickets stalled their soothing song.

Nothing else existed save for the two of them.

He held his breath.

Her eyelids fluttered.

Then the dreamy haze lifted as she cleared her throat. "I suppose we better get back to our dinner."

She propped herself up, prepared to leave the hammock.

But before she could grasp the overhead branch and ease herself back onto the deck, he grabbed her hand. "Wait."

His pulse throbbed in his ears and she met his gaze with an unreadable expression. "Thank you for sharing that with me. I know it wasn't easy. And I just want you to know that, as your friend, I'm here for you if you ever want to talk more about it."

Although he knew offering her only friendship was what she needed, the words tasted bittersweet.

He could only hope that when she was ready for more, he wouldn't miss his chance.

CHAPTER EIGHTEEN

*A*s Olivia traversed the footpath by the creek on her way home from Reed's, she realized she had no idea what time it was. The moonlight cast an incandescent gleam across the surface of the water making it appear lit from within. If she had to guess, she'd say the hour resided somewhere between nine and ten.

She suspected her parents would be wrapping up their evening of *M*A*S*H* reruns sometime soon. But as she crested the hill, she caught sight of her mother climbing out of the car dressed in a knee-length shift dress reminiscent of the 1920s.

"Costume party?" Olivia asked quietly, careful not to startle her.

"Book club." Harriet adjusted the cloche hat covering her bob of dark hair. "Ever since Sylvia took it over, she's established theme nights. Whenever we discuss a novel, we all have to dress in costumes suitable to the era. Even the snacks are period appropriate."

"Sounds fun. What book did you discuss tonight?" She fell in step beside her mother, surprised when Harriet paused at the top of the stairs without answering.

"It's such a lovely evening. Why don't we sit on the porch for a few minutes before heading inside?"

"Um..." Olivia hesitated. Exhausted after the emotionally taxing evening, she preferred to go straight to bed. Besides, sitting alone with her mother without an agenda other than idle chitchat would be unnecessarily risky. So far, she'd managed to avoid too many inquiries about Steven. "I'm actually pretty tired...."

"Two minutes," Harriet pressed, oddly intent on remaining outside. "The cool night air and soothing sound of the bullfrogs will do us both some good. Don't you miss it?"

"A little," she admitted as her mother settled on the wicker loveseat, patting the plush cushion beside her.

Olivia reluctantly joined her, but did her best to hide her misgivings, plastering on a smile.

They sat in silence for a few minutes, listening to the calming cadence of each rhythmic croak, like a provincial lullaby, and Olivia finally relaxed.

"It's called *White Lies and Lavender Lace*," Harriet said out of the blue.

"What?" Olivia asked, wrenched from her lulled state of tranquility.

"The book we discussed tonight. The author is Juliet Despereaux," she explained as though they'd never changed the subject. "It's based on a true story about a woman in 1920s England whose husband ran off with a courtesan, leaving his family and fortune behind. For three years afterward, the wife successfully kept his desertion a secret from everyone in town, supposedly to protect her family's wealth and reputation."

A sudden chill swept over Olivia and she suppressed a shiver. "Sounds interesting."

"It certainly made for a fascinating discussion. Although, it got a little heated when we debated whether or not she'd done the right thing."

Struggling to keep her tone calm and casual, Olivia asked, "And what did you think?"

"Truthfully, I'm not sure. After all, who am I to judge? But if I've learned anything from my mistakes, it's that honesty is generally the best policy."

Chewing her lip in thought, Olivia twisted the platinum ring around her finger. "Even if people get hurt?"

Harriet sat with her question a moment before replying. "Aren't people usually hurt by a lie, too?" she asked softly. "I suppose at some point, it's a choice between the lesser of two evils, isn't it?"

"I guess so," Olivia murmured, too drained to think straight.

"Come on, sweetheart." Harriet tapped her knee. "Time to get you to bed. You look exhausted."

As Olivia followed her mother inside, she had a sinking feeling that perhaps Harriet knew more than she let on.

*O*ver the next few days, Reed couldn't stop thinking about how Steven had stolen all of Olivia's clients, forcing her out of the business she'd built with her own two hands. It didn't sit well that the slimeball had gotten away with it. But what could he do?

Even as he contemplated his limited options, he had to admit that she seemed to be doing better than ever, as if sharing the rest of her secret with him had lifted a burden that had been holding her back.

Not only did she appear more joyful and content, but she'd actually joined him and the rest of the gang for dinner at Jack's one evening, laughing and joking like one of the group. She'd even met some of the women for coffee the following morning, without him needing to poke and prod her to go.

Like the miracle he'd prayed for since they were kids, she'd blossomed beyond his most hopeful expectations. And he couldn't help daydreaming about what it might mean for them in the near future. He'd even started planning how he wanted to finally confess all the feelings he'd kept bottled up for so long.

While he hadn't sorted out all of the details, he wanted it to be memorable.

Focusing on the present, he watched with a smile as Olivia glided around the Windsor property as though floating on air, showing off all their hard work to Grant and Eliza.

"And over here is where we'll set up the dance floor." She gestured toward an open patch of lawn, her countenance radiant. "Luke's constructing a wooden pergola to go around it. We'll string lights across the top and hang a chandelier in the center."

"I love it," Eliza gushed, clasping her hands in delight. "It's all even more beautiful than I imagined."

"Nice job, sis." While Grant gifted her with the compliment, he kept his gaze on his fiancée, clearly pleased to see her so thrilled.

"Reed helped a little." Olivia winked at him, and he nearly lost his footing. Fortunately, no one seemed to notice.

"You guys make a great team." Grant slapped him on the back. "Thanks for all the hard work you put into getting this place ready on time."

"Yes! We can't thank you enough," Eliza chimed in gratefully. "This wedding is going to be everything I hoped for and more. And it's all because of you two."

"Just doing my job," Olivia said humbly.

But Reed could see the pride shimmering in her eyes. She loved making people's dreams come true. And she was incredibly good at it.

Once again, his thoughts drifted to Steven and everything he'd taken away from her. But even if he could somehow fix it, and get back what was rightfully hers, would he want to? He might as well buy her a one-way ticket back to New York while he was at it.

"Where will we hold the ceremony?" Grant asked, surveying the huge backyard that presented several possibilities.

"I thought we'd use the gazebo as a backdrop," Olivia suggested. "But before we move on from the dance floor, there's one other idea I wanted to run by you." She drew in a deep breath before adding, "I know there isn't much time before the wedding, but instead of doing a traditional first dance, I thought it might be fun to… think bigger."

"What'd you have in mind?" Grant asked, tilting his head with interest.

"Have you two thought about choreographing something? With your dance skills, I bet you could come up with something really spectacular."

"What a fabulous idea!" Eliza squealed, bouncing on the balls of her feet. "Can we, Grant? It would be so much fun!"

A slow smile spread across his face. "It would be perfect. Honestly, I'm surprised we didn't think of it ourselves."

"You've both had a lot on your mind," Olivia offered. "There are so many details to plan, it's impossible to think of everything on your own. That's why you have me."

"Thank you, thank you." Eliza threw her arms around her, barely able to contain her excitement. "You seem to know what we want even better than we do."

Olivia laughed, returning her hug. "I'm just happy you're happy."

As Reed watched the exchange, his resolve solidified in his heart.

No matter the personal cost, he had to at least try to get her business back.

If he found a solution, he'd present it to Olivia and let her decide what she wanted.

At the very least, it should be her choice to make.

Even if it meant losing her again.

CHAPTER NINETEEN

*W*hen Reed called to say he'd be spending the day boating on Willow Lake for Grant's bachelor party, Olivia decided to take a drive.

After all those years of being chauffeured around the city, she realized she missed being behind the wheel. For some reason, it helped clear her thoughts.

And she had a lot to think about. Namely, what was she going to do with the rest of her life? Without her business bringing in income, she'd been burning through her savings, especially since she now shouldered the exorbitant rent for their swanky apartment.

While she'd thought about starting over in Poppy Creek, without Sanders Farm as a venue, she anticipated her event-planning services wouldn't be in high demand. She very much doubted that Jack and Kat would want to continue hosting events once the inn opened, since the commotion and hubbub would inevitably disrupt their guests who came to relax.

After winding along the quiet country roads, Olivia found herself on a familiar gravel driveway several miles outside of town. The rose-covered archway with a stained-glass sign announcing the entrance to Ciao Bella Garden awaited her approach.

Although the sprawling nursery was open to the public today, a small booth was set up near the gift shop and it appeared to be a book signing by a local author. She surmised the novel had a Parisian setting since the author—who wore a purple beret over her short-cropped hair—handed out macarons and fancy chocolates to each passerby.

Olivia observed the scene with a wistful longing, mulling over how wonderful it would be to own a place this idyllic and conducive to hosting so many different events.

"Hello! So nice to see you again." The warm greeting came from Isabella Russo, who strode toward her with a friendly smile. "Are you a fan of the author?"

"No, I…" She paused, deciding to answer honestly. "I was out for a drive and found myself turning down your road."

"This place does seem to have that effect on people," Isabella said with a silky laugh. "It's all of the flowers, I think. They attract more than the bees."

"You might be right." Olivia returned her smile. "You've also created such a charming environment. I could spend hours here."

"Well, if you ever want a job…" Isabella's lighthearted tone indicated that she wasn't entirely serious, considering for all she knew, Olivia still had her event-planning business in New York.

"Thanks. I'll keep that in mind," Olivia responded warmly, realizing the idea wasn't exactly terrible.

"It's a shame Poppy Creek doesn't have a place like this," Isabella said. "If Reed's nursery were a little bigger, it would make a beautiful venue."

"You've seen his place?" Olivia asked without thinking, immediately regretting her lapse in memory. Of course Isabella had seen it! What a ridiculous question.

Isabella flushed slightly. "We, uh… used to date a while back."

While Olivia already knew this information, she couldn't

squelch her overwhelming curiosity. And in a rare moment of boldness, she asked, "Do you mind me asking what happened? You two seem to have so much in common."

As if slightly embarrassed, Isabella glanced at the ground.

"I'm so sorry. That was rude and intrusive," Olivia said quickly, shocked by her own audacity. "Please ignore me."

"No, no. It's perfectly okay. I only hesitate because..." She lifted her gaze, a tentative glint in her dark eyes. "I wasn't quite sure how to explain it, but I always had this feeling that he was still in love with someone."

Olivia blinked in surprise. "Someone else?"

"Yes. Although I never asked him about it. We simply decided we'd be better off as friends. And while I can't lie and say I'm glad things didn't work out between us, I'm grateful to still have his friendship. He's truly one of a kind. But then, you already know that."

Something in her soft smile made Olivia's neck grow hot, but she wasn't sure why.

"I don't know about you," Isabella said brightly, shifting the mood, "but I'm dying for some chocolate. Care to join me?"

As Olivia accompanied her toward the author's booth, she couldn't help lingering on her words.

Reed had been in love with someone else....

Why did more than a little part of her wish to be that someone?

*a*fter a few hours of boating, the bachelor party relocated to the solitary pier on Willow Lake. Armed with coolers of ice-cold sarsaparilla—Grant's favorite licorice-infused soda—and a plethora of snacks courtesy of Jack's diner, they set up camping chairs near the middle of the walkway.

It didn't take long for Jack and Colt to start quibbling over who would catch the largest bass for dinner that night. The debate quickly devolved into who would prepare it the best, Jack championing his tried-and-true pan-fried recipe while Colt waxed poetic about his lemon herb butter and special searing method.

Luke and Grant merely watched the exchange with amusement, scarfing down the box of desserts Eliza had sent.

"You loudmouths are scaring away all of the fish," Reed chided, gathering his fishing pole and tackle box. "I'm going to set up shop farther down, so you can chase them my direction with all of your blabbering."

"Suit yourself." Colt shrugged, then added with a dimpled grin, "But you won't have much luck without me. The fish are drawn to my magnetic personality."

"It sure isn't your looks," Jack snorted, which instigated more boisterous bantering and good-natured insults.

"Gee, thanks for that," Luke grumbled, rolling his eyes.

"I'll save you a spot for when their bickering escalates to a cannonball competition," Reed offered with a chuckle. But as he situated himself at the end of the pier, balancing his pole in a knothole near the edge, he realized how badly he'd craved a moment of solitude to clear his head.

Reclining on the smooth pine slats in his board shorts, he closed his eyes, relishing the warmth of the sun on his exposed skin.

Before long, summer would be upon them, which meant longer days filled with boating, kayaking, swimming, and lazy afternoons soaking up all the vitamin D his body could handle.

Would Olivia be back in New York by then? And perhaps the bigger question, would he follow her there?

His thoughts drifted to the irrational idea he'd had for how to save her business. It had struck him in the middle of the night, keeping him awake for six miserable hours. While, so far, it remained his only option, he wasn't convinced it was his best one. Especially since it required asking for a cringeworthy favor.

When a cold, creamy substance landed on his bare chest, Reed jolted out of his reverie with a startled outcry. "Hey!" His eyelids rocketed open, and he saw Grant standing over him, a tube of sunscreen poised and ready.

"What are you doing?" Reed threw up his hands in defense.

"Sorry, but it had to be done," Grant told him, not sounding the least bit apologetic. "You've refused to wear sunscreen all day, and Eliza made me promise none of us would come back looking like boiled tomatoes."

"But I don't burn," Reed grumbled, sitting up to smear the glob of lotion across his torso.

"Better safe than sorry. Eliza doesn't want you ruining the wedding photos."

"Unless you had a last-minute wardrobe change, we'll be wearing a shirt with our suit and tie."

"Touché." Grant grinned, adding, "At least put some on your face. You don't want to upset the bride this close to the wedding."

"You have a point." Reed swiped a dollop onto his finger and applied it across his forehead.

"By the way," Grant said, sitting beside him on the pier. "It was cool seeing all the work you guys have done out at the Windsor Place. I know I said this before, but you and Olivia really do make a good team."

"Yeah, we do, don't we?" Reed answered with a twinge of pride. They'd accomplished a lot in a short amount of time.

"I hate to ask, but..." Grant studied the sapphire-hued surface of the water, not meeting his gaze.

"What?" Reed pressed, curious what was on Grant's mind.

His features pale and tense, Grant asked, "Is there something going on between you and my sister?"

Caught off guard, Reed gaped, his heart suddenly pounding in his ears. "W-what? Why would you ask that?"

"I don't know," Grant groaned, raking his fingers through his dark waves. "I don't even know *what* I'm asking, exactly. I know you'd never cross a line. It's probably not even about you, really. You guys are friends, and I get that. It's just..." He paused, struggling for the right words. "I'm worried something's off between her and Steven. But she won't talk about it. You know how she is, always trying to get through life on her own."

His stomach churning with guilt, Reed wasn't sure how to respond. He wanted to confess everything, to alleviate his own burden as well as his friend's. But the timing wasn't right, nor was it his secret to share. Instead, he offered the only assurance he could give. "Whatever's going on with her, I have no doubt she'll tell you the second she's ready."

Grant nodded slowly. "You're right. I guess after I spent all those years being caught up in my own stuff, not realizing what she was going through, I feel the need to make up for lost time."

"You're a good brother, Grant," Reed said with complete sincerity.

"Thanks. And not to lay on the schmaltz too thick," Grant said with a lopsided grin, "but you're a good friend. To me *and* Olivia."

"Hey, save the mush for your wedding vows," Reed teased, knowing his expression communicated his appreciation.

Although, his gratitude encompassed more than Grant's compliment. He'd given Reed the final push he needed.

The second he got home, he'd make the dreaded phone call to his father.

CHAPTER TWENTY

*A*fter her conversation with Isabella, Olivia had uncovered more questions than clarity.

Who had Reed been in love with all those years ago? And why, after all this time, did a hidden corner of her heart still long to be the woman he desired?

The yearning was almost laughable, considering her current state of scorn and rejection. She may have been remotely appealing at one brief point in time, but who would want her now that she'd been tainted by her divorce?

Certainly not someone like Reed, who could have a woman as incredible as Isabella.

Feeling utterly lost and hopeless, she decided to visit someone who'd been a pillar of kindness and inspiration since she arrived.

Eliza Carter, her soon-to-be sister-in-law, lived in a darling cottage on Walnut Tree Lane. The Victorian-style home with a cheerful red door and inviting front porch exceeded her brother's most florid and colorful descriptions. And the second she eased into one of the smooth rocking chairs, her anxiety started to slip away.

"Here you go." Eliza handed her an iced latte and a warm

chocolate chip cookie before settling in the rocking chair beside her.

The tantalizing and sugary scent teased a slight smile from her lips, as did the sweet, homey scene of Ben playing fetch with a scruffy, snaggle-toothed terrier a few yards away.

A paradise for child and grownup alike, the front yard boasted a sweeping walnut tree that created a generous canopy, shading the lush lawn dotted with winsome patches of clover and dandelions. Olivia imagined Ben had created many fond memories involving grass-stained jeans and hunting for elusive four-leafed clovers.

"Thanks for letting me barge in on your day off."

"Barge in anytime. We want to see you as much as possible before you head back to New York. Ben won't stop talking about his cool Aunt Olivia who used to have a pet possum."

Olivia's heart melted, filled with fondness for her nephew. "You've raised an incredible kid."

"Thanks." Eliza's gaze softened as she watched Ben tussle with Vinny over the blue rubber ball. "Of course, Grant deserves a lot of the credit, too," Eliza added with audible affection. "He's been wonderful this past year. So much so, I can't fathom how we ever got along without him."

Deep in thought, Olivia nibbled on the cookie before washing it down with a languid sip of the sweet, creamy concoction that contained a much-needed kick of caffeine. "I don't know how you two did it."

"Did what?"

"Moved beyond all of the heartbreak from your pasts."

"Ah…" Eliza leaned her head back, her countenance pensive. "To be completely transparent, it's been hard. But surprisingly, the toughest part wasn't forgiving your mom. Although, don't get me wrong, that's not always easy, either." She cracked a wry smile. "But the biggest struggle was letting go of my own shame, believing I could have a second chance with Grant. For the longest time, I felt too broken. Too *tainted*, for lack of a better word."

Her gaze fell to her sandal-clad feet, studying their rhythmic movement as they rocked back and forth, and Olivia's chest tightened, all too familiar with Eliza's clouded expression.

"Sometimes," Eliza murmured. "If I'm really honest, the lies still whisper in the back of my mind, telling me I don't deserve to move on, and I should wallow in my mistakes for the rest of my life. I have to repeatedly remind myself that I've been given grace, a gift no one can take away, not even my own insecurities." She paused and wrinkled her brow, as though sorting through her own admission. "Does that make any sense?"

"Yes," Olivia whispered, too overcome with emotion to elaborate, lest she break down entirely.

It was as if Eliza had reached inside the hidden recesses of her mind and read her most private and protected thoughts.

"But there is something that helps me remember," Eliza added, her voice lifting. "A quote I saw once. I don't remember who it's by, but I'll never forget what it said."

Olivia held her breath, anticipating something verbose and profound.

"'Every flower blooms through dirt.'" A slow smile spread across Eliza's face. "Don't you just love that?"

As Olivia mulled over the modest words, the mental image planted a seed deep within her soul, sprouting roots that reached beyond her pain. "It's beautiful."

For too long, she'd been stuck in the past, permanently marred by her divorce and the belief that she'd never bloom again, never be beautiful to anyone, but especially not to herself.

But in that moment, she saw a tiny sprig of hope—that one day she could finally escape the mire.

*A*s soon as Reed got home from the lake, he didn't even make it through the doorway before slipping out his phone.

Sitting on the edge of the deck, he swung his legs over the side and pulled up his list of contacts. Was he really going to do this?

Calling his dad was one thing, but asking for a favor from the woman who'd torn his family apart? He felt a little sick just thinking about it.

But his best shot at helping Olivia would require hiring a ruthless business attorney. And since he didn't have thousands of dollars for legal fees—or connections outside of his father—he had no choice but to enlist the aid of his least favorite person: his father's girlfriend, Candice Conway.

At least, Reed assumed they were still together. By the time he'd decided to speak with his father again, he couldn't bring himself to even mention her name, fearful that saying it out loud would change his mind about reconciliation.

I'm doing this for Olivia, he reminded himself as he tapped his father's number.

The unrelenting ring reverberated even louder than usual, and a mix of regret and relief washed over him when he heard his father's bland voice mail greeting.

"Hey, Dad. I was hoping we could talk. I need"—scrunching his eyes shut, he swallowed the lump in his throat—"a favor. From both you and Candice, actually. It's a legal matter. Call me back when you get a chance."

His palms clammy, he jabbed the End Call button before releasing the breath he'd been holding.

"Hi, honey!"

Startled, Reed flung the phone from his grasp. It sailed toward the ground, landing in a clump of grass by his mother's feet.

"Sorry, hon. Didn't mean to scare you. I hope it's not broken."

A bead of sweat sprang to his brow as she bent to pick up his phone. He prayed his father's number wasn't still visible.

"Would you look at that," she chirped. "These protective cases really work. Barely even a scratch." She mounted the steps, carrying a Tupperware in one hand and his phone in the other. "I made bran muffins this morning and I had a few extra."

His heart sank. She used to make his father bran muffins for breakfast—much to his dad's dismay. He'd never appreciated her attempts to keep him healthy. And for some reason, she continued to make a full batch, knowing she'd never eat them all on her own.

"Thanks." He reached for his cell, his heart stuttering when a text buzzed.

Let it be anyone but Dad, he silently pleaded.

Fortunately, she didn't even glance at the screen as she passed it to him.

"I brought some papaya for Nips, too," she said with a smile.

"You spoil him." Self-conscious, he clutched the phone to his chest, waiting for her back to turn.

"That's a grandmother's job," she teased, letting herself inside.

The instant she crossed the threshold, he stole a glance at the message.

You can have any favor you want, but let's discuss it in person. My place, tomorrow afternoon.

Reed heard his mother fussing around the kitchen, and it sounded like she was putting a kettle on for tea.

Riddled with guilt, he texted back, *See you then*, before stuffing his phone in his back pocket.

If his mother knew the reason for the favor, he had no doubt she'd be on board. She'd do anything for Olivia. But even so, he couldn't bring himself to confess his plan, knowing it would cause her pain.

For now, he'd keep it a secret.

From his mother *and* Olivia.

CHAPTER TWENTY-ONE

*T*he second Olivia parked at the Windsor Place, a text pinged on her phone.

After unbuckling her seat belt, she reached into the back seat for her cell, a smile lighting her face when she saw the sender.

It faded when she read the message.

I'll be out of town today, but plan on making up for it by working late tonight.

While she found it odd that he didn't give an explanation, she suspected he'd explain everything when he got back.

For now, she'd spend a few hours hanging the flower baskets they'd potted earlier.

They'd also brought over several pallets of perennials from the nursery that she could plant without needing direction from Reed.

Moments later, as she dug her hands into the velvety soil, she inhaled deeply, filling her lungs with the scent of warm honey wafting from the delicate white petals of the sweet alyssum. Sweat dampened her brow as the sun heated the nape of her neck, but she didn't mind.

Peace and contentment wrapped around her, and she happily lost track of time.

As she made her way down the row, she blinked as sunlight glinted off of her diamond ring.

Leaning back on her heels, she studied her left hand, caked in dirt. Specks of soil lodged between the tiny melee diamonds encrusting the setting. Perhaps she should have taken it off before she started—or worn gloves. But the precaution hadn't even crossed her mind.

Pinching the circle of cool metal, she twisted it around her finger.

Did it really matter if it got dirty? The marriage it represented had already been sullied.

At the thought, she expected a pang of grief to ripple through her like it usually did. But other than a subdued wistfulness, her emotions remained unchanged.

Her pulse fluttering, she slid the ring a few millimeters up her finger, stopping at her knuckle.

She exhaled slowly.

Then, gathering a deep, cleansing breath, she closed her eyes and yanked with all her might.

The engagement ring slipped past her fingertip with a burst of intensity.

Next came the wedding band.

When she opened her eyes, the rings rested in her palm and her finger lay bare.

The thin, pale line left behind contrasted sharply against her tanned skin and dirt smudges.

Unexpectedly, tears burned her eyes even though her heart felt oddly free.

Moving on would still have its hurdles, but for the first time, she truly believed she'd be okay.

*A*s Reed strode down the narrow, cracked sidewalk, the sound of ocean waves crashing against the shoreline floated on the salty sea air.

His parents had always talked about moving to the coast one day. While his mother loved Poppy Creek, she thought the change in scenery would be good for her artistic muse. Instead, his father had pursued that dream with someone else.

Striding up to the little blue bungalow, Reed pushed the somber thought aside.

He'd come for Olivia, not to dwell on the past.

When his father answered the door, Reed blinked, taken aback by his altered appearance. Gone were the few extra pounds around his midsection and his once-dark hair had grayed and appeared decidedly thinner. Though still handsome, his features were more drawn than before, with extra lines etched around his eyes and mouth.

For all the money he'd made in his business dealings and his attractive, youthful girlfriend, his father didn't look happy. And Reed wasn't sure whether to be pleased or saddened by the revelation.

"Hi, son." Bruce wavered, as though contemplating an embrace, then deciding against it. "Thanks for coming."

"Thanks for meeting with me." Recovering from his shock, Reed followed his father inside.

His home, at least, was neatly kept, if not particularly cozy or inviting. Besides the proximity to the beach, nothing about the place exemplified the type of wealth his father had garnered after selling his sports memorabilia business. Had he squandered everything already? Or maybe Candice had. She did seem like the type to prefer expensive things.

As they entered the modest kitchen, Bruce asked, "Can I get you anything? A cup of coffee? A bran muffin?"

Reed stopped short. Bran muffin? His gaze fell to the plate on the counter. Giant brown mounds with oatmeal flakes and walnuts protruding from the dry crusts peered up at him. They looked exactly like his mother's recipe. She used to have to practically force-feed his father every morning. Why on earth would he still be eating them?

"No thanks. I really just came to talk to Candice. Is she coming?"

"I'm afraid not."

Reed immediately bristled. He'd come all this way.... Why hadn't his father told him she wouldn't be here? It felt like a trap. "Is she busy?"

"Actually, son..." Bruce sighed, his shoulders slumped. "I haven't seen Candice in years."

"You broke up?" Reed couldn't believe it. Or maybe he could. They were a terrible match, but it only seemed right that if his father had ditched his mother for her, he should stick it out.

"The truth is, we were never together."

For a moment, all Reed could manage was a blank stare.

Finally, he barked, "What you are talking about? Of course you were." Indignation rose in his chest. "That's the entire reason you and Mom split up."

"No, it's not." Bruce shook his head sadly. "That's what you all assumed, and I didn't correct you."

"I don't believe this." Agitated, Reed dragged his fingers through his hair, ready to explode in anger and frustration. None of this made any sense.

"I understand why you're upset," Bruce began, but Reed wasn't having it.

"I doubt it," he snapped.

"Let me explain—"

"Why you lied?" Reed cut in, seething now. "Why you let Mom think you'd *cheated* on her?" The word tasted like bile in his mouth. "Do you have any idea what that did to her?"

Bruce winced, but Reed didn't care. "What possible reason could you have for putting her through that?"

His features blanched, his father could barely meet his gaze when he admitted, "Because I'd been unfaithful in other ways."

"What does that even mean?" Reed wasn't sure if he really wanted to know, but at this point, he might as well hear the whole truth.

"When you and Mark moved out, and it became just me and your mother in that tiny house, I... started to worry. We had so little in common as it was, and I feared all that time alone would slowly eat away at us, ending in inevitable misery and loathing."

"And you think walking out on her didn't have the same result?" Reed asked bitterly.

"I made a mistake." His father's confession escaped in a strangled rasp. "An awful, unforgivable mistake. I was a coward. And believe me, if I could go back in time and make a different decision, I would."

Reed opened his mouth to protest, but something in his father's eyes—a deep, penetrating sorrow—seared straight to his heart, softening him ever so slightly. "Why the lie?"

"I thought if your mother hated me as much as I hated myself, it would save her from the pain of missing me. Each day without her has been a misery I wouldn't wish on anyone."

As Reed listened, he couldn't deny the sincerity in his father's voice, and he wasn't sure how to respond. He could tell him that he suspected his mother had been just as miserable the last few years. And while a raw, wounded part of him wanted to pile on, he couldn't bring himself to do it. He didn't want to punish him any more than he had already done to himself.

"Why now?" he asked quietly. "You've gone all this time without telling me the truth."

"For years, I've been wrestling with whether or not to tell you. And when you asked for a favor from Candice, I thought God had given me the push I needed to finally do the right thing."

Recalling why he'd come, Reed suddenly felt even more conflicted. What would he do now?

"While I never crossed a physical line with Candice," his father confessed, "I did cross emotional ones. And eventually, she wanted more. That's when I broke things off. I'm working with Decklan Wells now. And he's agreed to meet with you. About the favor you need. And…" Bruce hesitated before adding, "About the money I want to give you."

"Money?" Reed's spine went rigid. He didn't want anything from his father, except for help on Olivia's behalf.

"Your mother wouldn't accept anything in the divorce. And I certainly don't find any joy in spending it. I want it all to go to you and Mark. At least, most of it. Minus my basic living expenses."

When Reed merely gaped, too stunned to speak, his father said, "Just think about it. For now, we can discuss the favor. I told Decklan we'd meet at the café on the pier."

As Bruce headed for his wallet on the console table by the back door, Reed noticed a striking painting on the wall above it— a self-portrait of a woman he recognized.

"Why do you have that?" His gaze darted to his father's face.

"Your mother's beautiful, isn't she?" Bruce murmured softly. "I have a lot of her work. The gallery in Primrose Valley calls me whenever she brings something new. But this one is my favorite."

Speechless, Reed observed the adoration in his father's glistening eyes.

Clearly, even after all these years, his dad still loved her.

And Reed wasn't sure how he felt about it.

CHAPTER TWENTY-TWO

*W*hile Olivia felt like she'd made personal progress, things with Reed seemed to be at a standstill, maybe even a step backward. She'd hoped he'd want to meet up after his impromptu trip out of town yesterday, but the evening had come and gone without so much as a phone call.

It wasn't like Reed to brush her off without an explanation, especially considering how much time they'd been spending together lately. But perhaps she was reading too much into it?

The moment Olivia saw the sign welcoming her to Primrose Valley, some of her apprehensions lifted. Surely, Reed would be glad to see her at the rose festival, even if he hadn't officially invited her. Or anyone, for that matter.

She'd never known Reed to be shy about his horticulture skills, but maybe she underestimated the importance of the competition. Either way, she wanted to show her support. Especially since she'd missed all the previous years.

As she turned onto Main Street, her breath caught at the beautiful sight. Rose garlands and wreaths adorned every shop on either side of the tree-lined thoroughfare, and festive streamers stretched through the branches. Each Victorian-era storefront boasted its own vibrant hue, from periwinkle to rose petal pink to daffodil yellow, making Main Street look like a bouquet of brightly colored blooms.

Olivia parked behind the art gallery and followed the lively music on foot, happening upon a community park a few yards off the main road.

More beautiful than any park she'd ever seen, the picturesque setting appeared to be the town's central hub, and a mirthful crowd of townspeople and tourists gathered on the lawn.

For a moment, she forgot all about the reason she'd come, mesmerized by the idyllic snapshot of small-town life.

An ancient oak tree provided ample shade from the late afternoon sun, and a quiet stream trickled past, where young children splashed about, cooling off on the particularly warm day. Folksy musicians performed in the bandstand, serenading families who mingled around picnic tables, sampling scrumptious-looking food from various vendors. The sweet scent of funnel cake and cotton candy filled the air, and Olivia also noticed more sophisticated fare like wine-and-cheese pairings and specialty olive oil tastings.

Apart from Isabella's nursery, Olivia had never visited Primrose Valley before, and she already adored it.

Completely enamored, she meandered through the merriment, soaking up the sights and sounds, while also keeping an eye out for Reed.

Near the edge of the lawn, she spotted a white tent with a banner announcing the annual rose competition. The instant she ducked inside, the heady floral aroma flooded her senses, as did the dramatic display of nearly every color imaginable, be it magenta, violet, coral, or vermillion.

Struck momentarily speechless by the striking tableau, she focused her attention on finding Reed, finally locating him at the far end of the tent near the judges' table.

When she caught his eye, she waved, surprised—and more

than a little confused—to see a look of alarm flash across his features.

*T*oo shocked to speak, Reed ignored the judge's inquiry about his hybridization techniques.

What was Olivia doing here?

As she crossed the tent, his heart jumped into his throat.

No, no, no....

This was bad. Like an unrelenting aphid infestation kind of bad.

If she saw the rose now, everything would be ruined. She'd instantly realize his feelings for her, and then what? How could he explain himself in a crowded tent of complete strangers?

He wanted the moment to be intimate. Memorable. *Special.*

She couldn't find out like this.

"Would you excuse me?" Without waiting for a response, he rushed to head her off.

"Surprise," she said with a shy smile, her inflection more indicative of a question than an exclamation.

"Hey, you didn't have to come." His voice sounded tight and constrained. Probably because his heart was still lodged somewhere in his esophagus.

"I know. But I haven't been to the festival before. And I wanted to support you."

Guilt walloped him in the gut and his temperature rose a thousand degrees. Tugging on his collar, he tried not to panic. "Thanks. That's sweet of you, but—"

He froze. But what? What could he say? He had no idea how to express why she couldn't be here right now, short of confessing everything in front of an unwanted audience.

Her smile faltered. "Is something wrong? Should I not have come?"

At the mixture of hurt and bewilderment on her face, the knot in his stomach cinched. This couldn't possibly get any worse....

"Reed!"

Wrenching his attention from Olivia's crestfallen features, he spotted Isabella gesturing for him to join her over by the judges' table, no doubt signaling they were done with their deliberation.

Turning back to Olivia, he noticed a strange shadow cloud her eyes as she glanced between them. "I should go," she said quietly, taking a step back.

"Wait," he blurted, reaching for her arm, afraid she'd leave but also terrified she'd stay. "I'll come with you. Just let me tell the judges."

She met his gaze. "Reed, I don't understand what's going on, but you need to be here. This competition is important to you. We can talk later."

"Liv," he murmured, completely at a loss for how to fix the impossibly deep hole he'd dug. All he knew was that she was far more important than the competition. "Let me come with you. We can get out of here and go get dinner somewhere."

"I can't. I have Eliza's bachelorette party tonight. I wasn't planning on staying long. Only a few minutes, really. I just wanted to..." She shrugged, clearly confused by the whole situation.

And Reed couldn't blame her. Maybe he should abandon his idea of the perfect moment and ask her to stay, letting the chips fall where they may? Without question, all of his options were abysmal.

Before he could decide, Olivia spoke. "Isabella is trying to get your attention. I think the judges need you. Honestly, Reed, it's okay. We can talk about this later. I need to head back to Poppy Creek soon, anyway."

She didn't wait for a reply before turning to go.

He watched in defeated silence as she walked away, glancing

over her shoulder one final time to say, "Good luck," before exiting the tent and disappearing from sight.

As he stood there, rooted to the spot in agonizing indecision, he had a sickening feeling that he'd just made a terrible mistake.

CHAPTER TWENTY-THREE

*A*s Olivia stood on Eliza's doorstep, she inhaled slowly to collect herself. Although she'd had the entire drive home, plus the time it took her to pack and change her clothes, she still hadn't been able to wrap her head around what happened at the rose festival.

She'd never seen Reed so rattled before, so out of character. And combined with his mysterious trip yesterday, she didn't know what to think.

Although he'd sent several texts, asking to talk as soon as possible, she'd had to delay their conversation until tomorrow, already committed for the rest of the evening.

A headache looming, she pressed her fingertips to her temple, gathering a few steadying breaths. She couldn't dwell on her relationship with Reed right now, no matter how torn she felt. She owed it to Eliza to be upbeat and present for the bachelorette party, as impossible as it seemed at the moment.

With a slow exhale, she smoothed the cotton fabric of her nautical-striped pajama set, suddenly self-conscious. She'd never been to a slumber party before and her insecurities brewed beneath the surface.

Squaring her shoulders, she raised her fist and rapped three times on the glossy red door.

Laughter and lively chitchat emanated from inside.

Footsteps sounded and seconds later, the door flew open. "Welcome!" Wearing flannel shorts and an oversize law school T-shirt, Cassie grinned broadly. "Everyone else is here, but the party is just getting started."

Cassie reached for the small carryall clutched in Olivia's left hand, ushering her across the threshold. "I hope you're not claustrophobic. With seven of us crammed in here, it's going to be cozy." She set Olivia's bag in the hallway with the others before leading her into the living room. "I offered to host at my house, but Eliza insisted we have it here so Luke didn't have to leave for the night. And Ben gets to have his own slumber party with Grant and Jack. There are guest rooms upstairs if you're more comfortable with that, but I think it'll be fun to all be squished together."

She laughed, and Olivia saw what she meant when they entered the living room. Air mattresses lined the floor at the foot of the couch, piled high with blankets and pillows. Eliza, Penny, Kat, Lucy, and Sadie sat cross-legged on the cushy mound sipping fruity-looking pink drinks in old-fashioned soda glasses.

"You're here!" Eliza squealed, carefully untangling herself from the blankets to greet her. She wore pink pajama pants and a matching tank top with *Bride* emblazoned on the front in sparkly gold glitter.

The other women set their drinks on the coffee table and joined her, instantly making her feel welcome and included.

"We're so glad you're here," Lucy told her with an enthusiastic embrace.

"And not just because Eliza wouldn't let us touch any of the snacks until you arrived," Penny teased, looking elegant in a 1940s-style nightgown.

"Yes, let's eat!" Eliza cheered. "I'm dying to get your opinions. We're sampling the dessert I want to serve at the wedding."

As they made their way into the kitchen, Olivia's curiosity piqued. When Eliza first mentioned the idea of a cookie dough bar, she wasn't entirely sold on the idea. She'd expected something more elegant and elaborate from a professional baker. But then, Eliza explained how she couldn't decide on one particular dessert, and that making cookies together—and devouring most of the dough before they were baked—had become a cherished memory between herself, Grant, and Ben.

Witnessing the look of love and affection that flickered across Eliza's face as she recounted the tradition, Olivia knew it was the perfect choice.

The women oohed and aahed when they entered the kitchen and caught sight of the beautiful presentation on the butcher-block island. Vintage parfait glasses with eggless cookie dough lined the counter surrounded by pink crystal dishes offering the most delectable toppings—white chocolate chips, macadamia nuts, toasted pecans, butterscotch candies, crushed chocolate-covered espresso beans, crumbled brownie bits, and so many more.

"There are three different choices for the dough," Eliza explained. "Classic chocolate chip, peanut butter, and Grant and Ben's favorite, tiramisu."

As the women built their customizable cookie dough creations, chatter turned to other wedding details, and how each one complemented both Eliza's and Grant's unique personalities.

Unbidden, Olivia's thoughts drifted to her own wedding. None of the elements chosen had been particularly personal. Steven had insisted they go with upcoming trends to show their guests that she had the pulse on the bridal industry. The entire event felt like a sales pitch rather than a meaningful celebration.

The irony was that she'd sacrificed her dream wedding to build someone else's business.

She glanced at her bare ring finger, knowing she couldn't use cleaning as an excuse forever. But now that she'd taken it off, she couldn't bring herself to slip it back on, almost as if it didn't belong to her anymore.

Or perhaps more accurately, as though she were an entirely different person.

If only she knew what the *new* Olivia was supposed to do with her life….

And how Reed fit into it.

*O*n his way home from the festival, it took all of Reed's concentration to focus on the road.

Not even winning the rose competition could steer his thoughts from how badly he'd blown it with Olivia.

He'd been so worried she'd find out about his feelings for her in front of countless strangers and prying eyes, he'd pushed her away—perhaps even ruined any chance for the future.

Somehow, he had to fix it.

Unfortunately, he would have to wait until morning since she had Eliza's bachelorette party that evening. Which meant he had all night to wallow in his mistake.

As he drove past his mother's cottage, he looked for her car in the driveway, hoping for a distraction, and maybe some advice.

Except, he got more than he'd bargained for.

Parked next to his mother's retro VW bug convertible, sat a familiar Studebaker wagon.

His heartbeat quickened as he pulled up alongside it.

He didn't even bother knocking as he strode inside, bracing himself for an unpleasant scene.

His mother glanced up, visibly surprised to see him. "Hi, honey." Her gaze darted from his stony expression to his father sitting beside her on the couch.

Bruce bolted to his feet, as though caught red-handed. "Reed, I stopped by your house, but you weren't home, so I..." He cast a furtive glance at Joan, who motioned for him to sit back down.

Reed studied his mother warily during the exchange. Her eyes weren't red or blotchy and she didn't seem uncomfortable or in any distress. In fact, she looked... almost happy.

"Join us, honey." She patted the cushion on her other side. "I set out some lemon bars and iced hibiscus tea. I'll get you a glass." Without waiting for his objection, she rose and walked to the kitchen, leaving them alone.

Struggling to keep his composure, Reed uncurled his fists, which he realized had inadvertently clenched at his sides. "What are you doing here, Dad?"

Bruce cleared his throat, leaning forward to grab a manilla envelope off of the coffee table. "I came by to give you this. When you weren't home, I decided to head back into town and wait at the new coffee shop, but your mother saw me driving by and invited me in." He handed Reed the envelope, his countenance contrite. "I honestly wasn't expecting it. I didn't think she'd ever want to speak to me again, let alone invite me in for tea."

Uncertain how he felt about the impromptu reunion, Reed slipped out the top sheet of paper, delaying his response. But the words jumbled on the page. He couldn't shake the image of his parents sitting side by side on the couch, a little too close for comfort.

"Decklan has laid out the necessary steps for Olivia to take legal recourse against her ex," Bruce explained. "But he doesn't think it'll ever go to court. He believes that once Steven sees this, he'll agree to give Olivia what he unlawfully stole. Otherwise, he's facing an enormous settlement and possibly jail time. His girlfriend, too."

His head swirling with an overwhelming amount of information to process, Reed stuffed the papers back inside the envelope. "Thanks for doing this."

"I'm happy to help. I've always liked Olivia. You know that."

Reed nodded, his throat suddenly tight as memories of the way life used to be—before both Olivia and his father left—flooded his mind.

"I'll go say goodbye to your mother and be on my way," Bruce offered gently, heading for the kitchen.

"Dad, wait." Reed crinkled the papers in his hand, wavering over his next words. Finally, he said, "You should stay."

"Really?" Bruce didn't hide his shock.

"Yeah. I'll go. And…" He paused and took a deep breath before adding, "You should tell Mom what you told me… about Candice."

"You think so?" His gaze flickered down the hallway, his expression uncertain, yet hopeful.

"Yeah, I do."

While Reed wasn't sure how his mother would react, she deserved to know the truth—all of it.

As did Olivia.

And sooner rather than later.

CHAPTER TWENTY-FOUR

*A*s she refilled her glass of raspberry lemonade in the kitchen, Olivia couldn't stop smiling.

She'd had such a wonderful time over the past few hours—a blissful respite from worrying about her awkward exchange with Reed earlier.

Lounging in the living room in their pj's, the women had laughed and conversed about anything and everything, all while painting their nails and devouring way too much junk food.

Olivia had always believed she'd missed her last opportunity for a good old-fashioned slumber party, but to her delight, she'd been wrong.

And the evening couldn't possibly get any better.

"Hurry, Liv!" Lucy called from the other room. "The show's starting!"

After plopping a handful of fresh raspberries into her glass, Olivia rushed to join the other girls, who eagerly awaited a reality show Eliza described as her guilty pleasure.

Although she'd never seen an episode herself, Olivia had heard all about *Dress Wars* from several of her clients. The show, filmed in New York City, awarded brides with the dress of their dreams, after they participated in theatrical and often humorous competitions staged in a famous bridal boutique.

Steven used to tease her that if the show had been around when they got engaged, she should have tried out for it, claiming the publicity would've been a huge boost for her business. Olivia simply smiled and went along with the joke, grateful she never had to endure the embarrassment.

As she entered the living room, all eyes were on the TV, and the show's tuxedo-clad host was already interviewing the first contestant.

The woman's icy gaze pierced through her, and Olivia instantly froze.

"Tell us," the host prompted from his perch on an ornate armchair in the lobby of the bridal boutique. "Why do you want to win today's competition?"

"That's easy," the woman responded smugly, her unctuous smile seeping through the television screen. "My fiancé deserves to see his bride in the most beautiful dress imaginable on his wedding day. His first bride was a bit of a disappointment, if you know what I mean." She puffed out her cheeks like a blowfish while circling her arms to indicate an extra-large midsection, then cackled as though she found herself hilarious.

Scorching heat swept across Olivia's entire body and all the oxygen seemed to leak from the air. She wanted to run or sink into the floor, but remained paralyzed by her own mortification.

"Yikes, she's awful." Lucy wrinkled her nose in distaste.

"Some of the women are total bridezillas," Eliza admitted. "But now we know we're rooting for her rival to win."

The other girls adamantly vocalized their agreement.

"And who is the lucky groom?" the host prodded, clearly relishing the drama.

Olivia's heartbeat raced out of control, but she couldn't move, couldn't speak. A voice in her head screamed for someone to turn off the TV, but her words were trapped in her raw, constricted throat.

The woman appeared to look directly at her as she announced with a haughty smirk, "Steven Rockford III."

A loud crash muffled the collective gasp of shock as everyone spun in her direction.

Pink sugary liquid and shards of glass pooled at Olivia's feet and her now-empty hand shook uncontrollably.

Overcome with shame and humiliation, she resisted the hot tears threatening to spill down her cheeks. Her perfect night had turned into a nightmare—disgraced in front of her new friends, not to mention the revelation of her horrible secret. She could only imagine the scorn and ridicule to follow.

Suddenly dizzy and overwrought, her knees buckled, but Eliza and Lucy were already on their way, there to catch her before she joined her raspberry lemonade on the parquet floor.

Each looping an arm around her waist, they carefully led her around the broken glass to the couch, where all the women gathered around her, gently voicing their care and concern.

Seconds later, someone handed her a box of tissues while Eliza rubbed her back with soft, motherly attention as the tears fell unrestrained.

In that moment, something shifted in Olivia's heart.

The shame faded, along with her fear, as she realized these women were offering her something rare and precious—their unconditional love.

And she had a choice.

She could run away or let them in, owning all of her messiness and scars.

Taking a deep, quivering breath, she decided to bare it all, trusting that some risks were worth taking.

*P*acing across the knotted pine floor, Reed glanced at the wall clock for the billionth time while Nips bobbed back and forth on his perch, as though joining him in spirit.

"What do you think?" Reed asked. "It's nine in the morning. Do you think Olivia will be back from the bachelorette party yet?"

Nips ruffled his feathers.

"Yeah, you're right." Reed straightened his shoulders. "I should just go over there and find out."

Truthfully, he didn't think he could wait any longer. As soon as he'd resolved to tell Olivia everything, perfect moment or not, he hadn't been able to eat, sleep, or do much of anything.

Even Nips seemed to absorb some of his nervous energy, flitting about the tree house at all hours of the night.

Striding to the table, Reed reached for the manilla envelope and tucked it beneath his arm before grabbing the larger, heavier item draped in a swath of white fabric.

It took some effort to cross the creek and maneuver up the steep embankment with his arms full, but he persevered, focused on his mission—to once and for all tell Olivia how he felt about her.

He'd buried the truth for so long, fighting his feelings with an exhausting determination, the thought of finally confessing everything left him more breathless than the physical exertion.

Of course, he knew she might turn him down, and the possibility hung around his neck like a burdensome yoke. And yet, for the first time in years, the urge to take a chance on something worthwhile outweighed his doubts and trepidation.

He'd lost Olivia once, too afraid to put his heart on the line.

But this time? He'd go all in.

By the time he reached the Parker residence, his forearms ached, and he couldn't wait to relinquish his load.

As he searched the driveway for Olivia's rental car, he caught sight of Harriet kneeling before a bed of red and violet impatiens. She glanced up when she heard him approach. "Good morning, Reed. What brings you by on this lovely day?" Leaning back on her heels, she smiled up at him beneath her floppy-brimmed hat.

"Good morning, Mrs. Parker." His heartbeat thrummed a bit faster as he asked, "Is Olivia home?"

"I'm afraid not. Is that for her?" She eyed the bulky object in his arms.

"It is." He hesitated, unsure of his next move. Should he come back later? Disappointment swelled in his chest at the thought of waiting a second longer.

"You're welcome to leave it inside, if you'd like," Harriet offered. "I don't expect her back for another hour, at least."

Again, he wavered. There really wasn't a perfect solution.

Drawing in a deep breath, he reminded himself that he'd given up the notion of *perfect*, trading it for immediacy.

"That would be great, thanks."

As he headed for the door, Harriet rose to her feet and scurried ahead, holding it open for him. "She's staying in her old room," she told him with another smile before heading back to her gardening.

Reed's pulse rose with each step as he ascended the staircase, knowing that once he left his gift for Olivia to find, there would be no going back.

He slid it onto the dresser before gently removing the cloth covering.

The vivid, velvety petals seemed to unfurl with extra flair, as though they knew the important role they played.

His entire future hinged on what Olivia thought of this single rose.

CHAPTER TWENTY-FIVE

*S*hortly after nine, Olivia pulled up to her parents' home, an odd blend of nervous energy and steadfast resolve.

While most of the women lingered after breakfast, Olivia thanked everyone and left early, compelled to speak to her mother as soon as possible. Now that so many people knew her secret, it didn't feel right to keep her family out of the loop a second longer than necessary.

But as she sat in the driveway, she couldn't bring herself to exit the car.

Eliza had been nothing but compassionate and kind, assuring her that she hadn't soured the wedding in the slightest. She seemed more concerned with making sure Olivia was okay than anything else. In fact, Eliza and the other women had listened and comforted her most of the night. By the morning, she felt renewed and emotionally stronger than ever before, bolstered by their wise, reassuring words and unwavering friendship.

Although her mother had grown a lot over the past year, Olivia wasn't convinced she'd handle the news with as much grace as Eliza.

For Harriet Parker, her daughter's flawless facade meant

everything. And in one fell swoop, she'd tumble off the pedestal her mother had so carefully crafted.

Gathering her courage, she slipped from the driver's seat.

As Olivia stole along the footpath, her mother kept her head down, busy weeding a patch of hardy English lavender in the front yard. Like an image straight off the pages of a gardening catalogue, Harriet knelt on a foam cushion, her pristine wardrobe free of wrinkles and without so much as a speck of soil.

Hearing Olivia's footsteps on the stone path, she glanced over her shoulder. "Hi, sweetheart. I wasn't expecting you home so early. Did you have a nice time?"

"I did." Olivia knelt beside her, not caring if she got dirt on her jeans. "But I really need to talk to you."

Slipping off her gloves, Harriet pushed up the brim of her hat, her gaze tender. "I was wondering when you would."

Olivia's eyes widened. "You know what I'm going to say?"

"About you and Steven?" Harriet asked gently. "I've suspected for a while now. But sweetheart, you haven't exactly been subtle the last few days. You left your rings in the ultrasonic cleaner for so long, I had to fish them out myself."

Her cheeks flushed, and Olivia glanced at her bare finger. The thin line had already started to fade, thanks to all her time in the sun. "I'm so sorry I didn't tell you sooner."

"Why did you feel the need to keep it from me?" Her mother's tone wasn't accusatory, but soft and slightly hurt.

Olivia's shoulders slumped, and she couldn't bring herself to meet her mother's gaze. "I guess... because I was ashamed that I'd let you down."

"Oh, Livy," Harriet breathed, taken aback by her daughter's admission.

"I liked being someone you were proud of," Olivia confessed, fresh tears burning her eyes. "My entire childhood, I was a colossal disappointment. And now that you thought I was no longer that girl anymore, I couldn't admit to you, or anyone, that I hadn't changed. That I was still the same easy target, an embarrassment you sent away, hoping to fix."

When Olivia finally summoned the courage to look her mother in the eye, she straightened in surprise.

Inky black mascara streaks marred her mother's red, blotchy cheeks. "I'm so deeply sorry, sweetheart," Harriet whispered.

"Mom, it's okay. I didn't mean to—"

"No, this needs to be said." Struggling for composure, Harriet placed a hand over Olivia's. "I will always regret not being the mother you deserved. I was a bitter, selfish person who prioritized all the wrong things. The way I treated you, the way those other girls in school treated you, had nothing to do with you." She squeezed her hand to emphasize her assertion. "Absolutely nothing. Our actions stemmed from the ugliness inside our own hearts. And I should never have let you carry that burden for all these years."

Her own tears rolled down her face now, but Olivia didn't wipe them away. They seemed cleansing somehow, as did her mother's words.

"I'm so sorry, sweetheart. I owed you this apology a long time ago."

Olivia placed her free hand over her mother's, and the two women cried silent tears together as years of pain sprinkled the dirt, soaking into the forgiving soil.

Sniffling, Olivia dabbed her damp cheeks, managing a small smile. "I could use another cup of coffee, if you want to hear more about what happened."

"I would love that. But first, there's something you should know. Reed stopped by earlier and left you something upstairs in your room."

"He did?" Olivia's gaze flew to her bedroom window. They hadn't spoken since their strange interaction yesterday. What could he have possibly brought her?

"He's a good man," Harriet said with touching conviction.

"Yes, he is…." Olivia hesitated.

She'd never admitted the truth to herself, let alone another living soul.

But she couldn't escape it.

She loved Reed, with every breath she possessed.

In all likelihood, she always had.

But what if they went down that road and both wound up hurt beyond repair?

"Love takes faith," Harriet told her, as though reading her thoughts. "It's a lot like tending these flowers." She gestured toward the bed of fragrant purple sprigs. "I did all the research beforehand, selected the right seeds and prepared the proper soil. I planted them, watered and nurtured them to the best of my ability. Then I had to step back and trust that they'd bloom."

The simple metaphor proved to be exactly what Olivia needed to hear, and she threw her arms around her mother, pulling her close.

There, kneeling in the soft dirt surrounded by the heady scent of lavender and the warmth of the morning sun, Olivia resolved to finally plant new roots.

And this time, she had faith they would last.

*H*er heart thrumming, Olivia hurried into her bedroom, uncertain what she'd find.

Her gaze immediately fell on a large ceramic pot on the dresser.

A gasp escaped her lips as she drew closer.

Covering her mouth with both hands, she stared at the most stunning rose she'd ever seen. Appearing to be a hybrid between a Sterling Silver rose and something else she couldn't quite place, its silky petals shimmered a familiar shade of violet blue with a lavender luster.

She lifted her gaze to her reflection in the mirror, her eyes glistening as she beheld the startling resemblance.

It must have taken Reed years of effort to perfect the hue... but why? Why did he do it?

Even as her subconscious asked the question, her heart knew the answer.

Reed loved her, too. Why hadn't she noticed before?

Or perhaps she had, but hadn't possessed the self-confidence to believe it.

Tears sprang anew, but this time they were tears of joy.

After so much heartache, she'd been given an incredible gift— a chance to love again. And to be loved and cherished in return.

Her heart almost burst with happiness.

Rushing out the door, she had only one thought in mind.

Find Reed.

CHAPTER TWENTY-SIX

oo restless to head back home after leaving Olivia the rose, Reed stopped at the creek to collect his thoughts. He wasn't sure how long he'd been standing there, tossing pebbles into the cool water, when a breathless voice called his name.

As he spun around on the bank of the stream, he saw Olivia hasten down the hill toward him, like a vision he'd dreamt about for so many years.

Her long dark hair fluttered behind her and her eyes—those enthralling, ethereal eyes—remained fixed on his as she kicked off her cumbersome sandals, quickening her pace.

He held his breath, every nerve in his body on fire as she neared, a smile illuminating her features.

She'd seen the rose. That had to be it.

His heart swelled with hope, both nervous and eager to hear what she had to say. But based on her exhilarated expression, he had a pretty good guess.

His skin tingled all over at the thought.

Then, the final breadth of her descent, something changed.

Her smile transformed to a stunned gasp as she lost her footing.

With only a few seconds to react, Reed held out his hands, hoping to catch her and break her fall. But as she careened into his chest, the force sent them both flailing backward into the creek.

Reed landed on his backside in the frigid water, Olivia on top of him.

To his surprise, she burst into laughter.

He joined in, imagining how ridiculous they must look.

But as quickly as the laughter began, it halted in her throat.

Her fingers splayed against his chest; he could almost feel the heat from her touch beneath his damp T-shirt.

Their mouths hovered mere inches from each other, and before he knew what was happening, she'd pressed her lips against his, sweetly at first, then more fiercely.

Reed matched her urgency, his need growing with each passing second, completely lost in the euphoria of finally knowing she wanted him, too.

The icy water, protruding rocks, and uncomfortable position, none of it mattered as he held Olivia in his arms and tasted her lips, which were so much sweeter than he'd ever imagined.

For most of his life, he'd believed this moment was impossible. Now, faced with the blissful reality, he struggled to breathe, overwhelmed by the intensity of his emotions.

When they finally parted, Olivia murmured, "I love you, too," and the sound nearly broke him, like a branch budding with more than its share of blossoms.

The woman he'd loved his entire life loved him in return. Could one person even handle that much happiness? He wasn't convinced he could. His chest ached, nearly bursting with immeasurable joy.

"I love you, Olivia," he murmured back, his voice raw and husky. "I always have."

She gazed into his eyes, searching. "Always?"

"I knew for sure shortly after you left for boarding school."

"Why didn't you ever say anything?" She straightened in surprise.

"I almost did."

Still craving her nearness, he scooted onto the embankment and drew her to his side. With her head nestled in the crook of his shoulder, the scent of her floral shampoo smelled even stronger on her damp hair. "I flew out for your college graduation, planning to tell you everything. How I'd been in love with you for years. How I'd built the tree house."

"I had no idea you were at my graduation," she whispered, sliding closer as though worried he might slip away again.

"I had no idea you and Steven were so serious," he admitted, still pained to recall the moment he'd stumbled on the truth. "When I got there, he was down on one knee. Talk about bad timing." He attempted a rueful smile, but couldn't quite manage it. To him, there was nothing funny about that day. "I wish I'd stayed and fought for you. And I won't make that mistake again." He reached for her hand, longing for the connection. "I know you're still going through a lot, and may not be ready yet. But I wanted you to know how I felt, and that if there was a chance you felt the same way, I'd wait for you, no matter how long it takes."

Her eyes glistening, she laced her fingers through his, and for the first time, Reed noticed she no longer wore her ring. As he traced the faded line, his already racing heartbeat thrummed ever faster.

"Thank you," she said softly. "I never imagined I'd get another chance at love, not to mention with the most amazing man I've ever met." Her voice broke, and he leaned his head against hers, desperate to kiss her again, but sensing she had more to say.

"But you're right," she added with a note of regret. "I do have some things to work through still. So, I'd like to take things slow. With you. Here in Poppy Creek."

She tilted her chin and met his gaze, and the gleam in her eyes told him everything he needed to know. He lowered his mouth to hers.

The slow, tender kiss sent him reeling, and he had no idea if a second passed or an hour.

Eventually, she pulled away to catch her breath, but Reed left his fingers gently cupping her face. He never wanted to let go. And when she smiled up at him, his heart soared.

Then, to his dismay, it slowly drifted back to earth when he remembered the manilla envelope resting on a rock by the water's edge. "As badly as I don't want to move from this spot, there's something I need to show you."

After retrieving the envelope, he settled beside her again, as close as humanly possible.

Ignoring the resistant clench in his fingers, he handed her the packet that could change everything.

"What's this?" She curiously opened the seal and slid out the top sheet of paper, staring at the jumble of legalese with a look of confusion.

He cleared his throat, suddenly worried the gesture might be too much. "The other day, when I was out of town, I went to see my dad and his lawyer. I told them about Steven and your assistant and what they did to your business."

Startled, she met his gaze, but she didn't look angry or upset, and he pressed on, momentarily relieved. "No one was contacted and no paperwork was filed. It's your decision. But my father's lawyer believes you have legal recourse to get your business back, if you want it."

She glanced at the papers again, tears welling in her eyes. "I can't believe you did this for me."

"I'm on your team, Liv," he told her, wishing he could adequately express the full extent of his words. "And whatever you choose to do with this, I support you. And if that means going back to New York, we'll figure something out. Because I don't want to lose you again."

In silent accord, she leaned into him, and he wrapped both arms around her, drawing her against his heart.

While the days ahead would be fraught with uncertainty, to Reed, the future had never been clearer.

$\mathcal{D}$uring the past twenty-four hours, Olivia still hadn't decided what to do about the paperwork from Reed's father's attorney.

Truthfully, she found it nearly impossible to focus. Her thoughts were consumed by one thing and one thing only—Reed Hollis.

And, more specifically, his heart-stopping kisses.

Subconsciously, her fingertips grazed her mouth—where he'd left a lasting impression—as she questioned how she could possibly think coherently in this frame of mind.

She'd hoped the change in scenery of The Calendar Café, and an extra-large White Rose and Lavender Mocha, would shake some sense into her. But even with her eyes wide open, the image of Reed drenched from head to toe, lowering his lips to hers, had been burned into her brain, for better or for worse.

It wasn't likely she'd get anything done today, let alone plan her future.

"Pastry for your thoughts?" After setting a warm cinnamon roll on the table, Cassie slid onto the chair across from her.

Olivia flushed, embarrassed to be caught daydreaming. Although she could really use a listening ear. "Just mulling over life-altering decisions," she confessed in a partial truth.

"Those are my favorite kind," Cassie said, her eyes twinkling. "Can I help?"

Trusting Cassie completely, she shared, "There's a lawyer willing to help me get my business back from Steven and Emily, if I want it."

"And do you?" Cassie asked simply.

"That's the thing..." Olivia toyed with the handle of the tall, transparent glass. "I'm not sure anymore."

"Is there something you *do* want?"

"Well..." Olivia stalled. She wasn't entirely ready to divulge what had happened between her and Reed. But she did know one thing for certain. "I don't want to live in New York anymore. I want to stay here."

"Then why don't you?" Cassie smiled, clearly not seeing the issue. "We'd all love for you to stay."

"Unfortunately, it's not that simple." Olivia sighed, unsure how to explain her dilemma. "For one thing, I don't have a viable way to make an income here. But more than that, a part of me wonders if I should stand up to Steven for what he did. I don't want to sue or spend years in court or anything. But I didn't push back at all. Maybe I let him win too easily?"

Cassie contemplated this a moment, then asked, "Are there only two options? Stay here and let Steven win, or go back to New York and stand up for yourself?"

"I-I don't know..." Olivia faltered.

"Maybe you need to find a third option." Cassie stood and reached for Olivia's mug. "I'll get you a refill while you think about it."

As Cassie strode toward the espresso machine, Olivia mulled over her words, an idea forming in the back of her mind.

This town had done so much for her....

Maybe there was a way to do something in return? Something that would change everyone's lives for the better. And allow her to stay here, with Reed, exactly where she belonged.

CHAPTER TWENTY-SEVEN

*O*ver the next few days, Reed did everything he could to give Olivia the time she needed to think things through. But it wasn't easy. Every time he saw her, he wanted to wrap her in his arms and cover her in kisses.

After waiting a lifetime, taking things slow really tested his self-control.

But she had a lot on her mind between deciding her future and pulling together the final details for the wedding.

And as Reed sat in his mother's front garden holding a large check in his hands, he had to face reality—Olivia wasn't the only one with a huge decision to make.

In fact, monumental changes seemed to be on the horizon for everyone lately, including his parents.

Ever since Bruce arrived with the papers for Olivia, his parents had started spending time together. His dad had come clean about everything, apologizing to his mother, Reed, and his brother, Mark, in turn.

While it was taking Reed and his brother a bit longer to let go of the past, Joan had never been more vibrant and effervescent, as though she'd suddenly become twenty years younger.

Reed straightened in the wicker lounge chair as she emerged from the cottage carrying a tray of iced tea and apple slices dipped in dark chocolate.

"Well?" she asked, sliding the afternoon snack onto a small table made out of recycled milk crates. "Are you going to keep it?"

"I haven't decided," Reed answered honestly.

"Honey," she said softly, sitting beside him. "You'll have to forgive your father eventually."

"Forgiveness is one thing. But moving forward, letting him back into my life... that feels different." He turned to face her. "How can you give him another chance after everything he put you through?"

"He's not the same man he used to be."

"And how can you be sure of that?" Although he wasn't trying to be argumentative, he needed to understand how she found it so easy to trust again.

"I can see it in his eyes." With that, she poured herself a tall glass of tea from the pitcher, adding a mint leaf and lime wedge for good measure.

Reed smiled. While his mom had a funny way of doing things, she was usually right. He glanced at the check. "So, you think I should accept the money?"

"I think your father believes you'll put it to better use than he ever could. And I have to say, I agree."

Reed let her words sink in, wondering what he would do with the check if he cashed it.

But before the question had fully formed in his mind, he realized he knew exactly what he wanted to do with it. He just wasn't sure if it was possible.

He thought of Olivia and the unbelievable kiss they'd shared in the creek. That had seemed impossible, too. Maybe he needed to stop worrying about the odds, get out of his own way, and go for it.

"Mom, do you mind if I take a rain check on the tea?"

"Not at all, honey."

Springing from the chair, Reed planted a kiss on her forehead. "Wish me luck."

Without asking for more details, she merely smiled. "You don't need it."

Chuckling softly, he hurried toward his van, hoping she was right.

As Reed turned down the lane to Sanders Farm, his heart raced erratically.

He'd heard the new owner had come to take a final walk-through before escrow closed, and he planned on changing their mind.

The entire drive from his mother's cottage, he'd rehearsed what he wanted to say, formulating a plea on the town's behalf. Perhaps if they knew how much the property meant to the people of Poppy Creek, they'd be willing to let him buy it instead. He'd even offer to pay the deposit, plus extra for their trouble.

Although he might wind up joining Olivia in New York, Reed hated the thought of his friends and family losing such an important fixture. The farm had hosted most of the town's major events since its founding. And now that he had the money to buy it, he had to at least try to save it.

In his haste, Reed didn't even bother driving all the way around to the parking lot. Instead, he screeched to a halt at the foot of the hill and sprinted up the steep incline, heading straight for the enormous red barn.

When he caught sight of Mitch Sanders exiting through the doorway, his heart rate surged.

"Mitch! Thank goodness I caught you," he panted. "Is the new owner here?"

"Yep! Still inside." Mitch grinned, appearing unusually giddy.

Reed's spirits faltered, but he'd come too far to quit now. "Mind if I talk to them?"

Mitch cocked his head, genuinely curious. "What for?"

"I want to buy the farm," Reed announced, hoping he sounded more confident than he felt in the moment. The stakes were too high to crumble, and he'd promised himself on the drive over that he wouldn't surrender until he'd given it his best shot.

Mitch lowered his bushy eyebrows in confusion. "But I already sold it. For more than the asking price, too."

"I know. But I'm hoping if I talk to them I can change their mind. You won't lose a dime, I promise. I'll offer the same amount, if not more."

"It's not just about the money," Mitch drawled, running a hand through his sandy hair. "I like the new owner. And I think this sale will be great for the town. But if you want to talk to her, you go right ahead." He headed toward the parking lot on the other side of the slope. "I'll be at Jack's. You two sort it out and let me know."

Reed watched him go, momentarily stunned. Mitch liked the new owner? How could that be? Didn't he know they wanted to turn the place into a private retreat and keep the town from using it ever again?

Confounded, he strode toward the barn, wondering if the rumors had been a mistake. Yanking open the solid pine door, he stepped inside, blinking as he adjusted to the change in light.

A tall, dark-haired woman stood in the center. She turned when she heard him enter.

Reed nearly fell backward when a slow smile spread across her face. "Olivia? What are you doing here?"

"I could ask you the same question," she said with a laugh.

"I came to try and buy out the new owners."

Her smile widened. "Guess I beat you to it."

"What do you mean?" Reed continued to stare, as if any

second he'd discover that he'd hallucinated the whole thing. He *had* been daydreaming about her nonstop.

"I convinced the original buyers to let me buy it instead," she explained, her voice bubbling with excitement. "A little unorthodox, but I made it worth their while. And Mitch couldn't have been more thrilled when I told him I wanted to turn it into an event venue."

"Hang on." Reed ran a hand along his jawline, trying to wrap his head around what she was telling him. "You bought this place?"

"Yep." She beamed, glowing with happiness. "I would have told you sooner, but I just received the money from Steven a few hours ago. I knew the buyers would be here today for their final walk-through, so I raced over. It all happened so quickly."

He took a step toward her, his pulse quickening as her words sank in. "The money from Steven?"

"Yes, that's the most surprising thing of all." Her eyes shone with a mixture of joy and disbelief. "I decided to call him about the paperwork from your father's lawyer. He caved so fast I couldn't believe it. Turns out, he doesn't have much of a spine, after all." She flashed an impish grin "I told him I didn't want the business back, but he should pay me what it's worth. We settled on a price, and he wired me the money this afternoon."

He knew how difficult it must have been for her to call Steven, and his chest swelled with pride. Without thinking, he closed the gap between them and scooped her into his arms. Pressing his lips to hers, he communicated what only his heart could say.

His entire body melted as she draped her arms around his neck, threading her fingers through his hair.

In that moment, he realized he could kiss her for an eternity and it still wouldn't be enough.

Parting too soon, she murmured, "There's more."

"How is that possible?" he asked in a low growl, desperate to capture her mouth again. "You just told me you're staying in Poppy Creek. It can't get any better than that."

She laughed softly against his lips. "I was wondering if you'd be interested in tearing down the property line and expanding the nursery. You could manage the grounds while I run the venue. What do you think?"

His answer came in the form of a kiss so intense, she folded against him.

Breathless, she gasped, "Please tell me we can end all of our business meetings like this."

"I'll put it in writing," he promised, hardly able to believe his best friend would now be his business partner.

And, he prayed, one day his wife.

CHAPTER TWENTY-EIGHT

*H*er heart full, Olivia smiled as she surveyed her handiwork. Without a doubt, this was her favorite wedding yet.

The plethora of fragrant, colorful blooms provided most of the charm, but the stunning pergola over the dance floor, draped in lights and flowering garlands, added to the whimsy. So did the elaborately decorated gazebo with gossamer drapery and a floral swag of eucalyptus, pink and white dahlias, and vintage-blue roses.

Flowers flourished everywhere, from the centerpieces decorating the long farm tables to the backs of each antique wooden chair awaiting the ceremony. Every detail, down to the buds and blossoms adorning the dessert table, embodied the beauty and romance of springtime.

Of course, she hadn't done it all on her own. That morning, half the town had arrived to help. Almost more hands than she knew what to do with, but she'd been grateful.

"Everything looks incredible." Lucy appeared by her side dressed in a gorgeous pale-blue gown. All of the bridesmaids wore the same romantic hue reminiscent of hydrangea petals. It looked especially pretty on Lucy, complementing her blond hair and light-blue eyes.

"Thanks. I couldn't have done it without everyone's help."

"I don't know," Lucy said with an admiring inflection. "You probably could have. You've always seemed like the kind of person who could do anything."

"Thank you, but I don't know about that."

A nostalgic smile stole over Lucy's features. "Growing up, Sadie and I thought you were the coolest girl in town."

"Me?" Olivia's eyes widened.

"Yes, you." Lucy laughed. "You were so different from everyone else, but in the best possible way. You know, after you moved here, Sadie and I didn't wear shoes for the entire summer."

"Really?" Now it was Olivia's turn to laugh. Her mother would've been horrified to know her unladylike habit had rubbed off on someone else's daughters.

"Yep. And I never forgot how kind you were. I still remember the time Jimmy Hanson dug up all the daffodils along the school-yard fence. You spent hours after school replanting them with your bare hands."

Heat swept across Olivia's cheeks as she recalled the memory. "I didn't realize anyone saw that."

"I did. And I always looked up to you because of it, even though I was too chicken to say anything."

"I had no idea," Olivia murmured, stunned that she'd had an impact on Lucy all those years ago.

A part of her wished she'd known. Even though she was a few years older, perhaps they could have been friends? But then, that's probably why she hadn't noticed Lucy or Sadie back then. She'd closed herself off, too afraid for history to repeat itself. Too afraid to see that kindness still existed.

"Just goes to show we never know whose lives we touch," Lucy said softly.

Olivia's throat tightened as gratitude washed over her. She couldn't go back and change the past, but she could be forever thankful that they were friends now.

She grabbed Lucy's hand and gave it a squeeze before they both turned at the sound of Cassie calling her name.

"Are you busy?" Cassie asked from the back porch. "Eliza would like to see you."

"The bride beckons you," Lucy said with a teasing lilt. "I'm going to go sign the guest book before people start arriving."

As Olivia strode toward the inn, she summoned her most confident event-planner poise, bracing herself for whatever had gone wrong.

Olivia slipped into the sitting room they'd converted into the bridal suite for the afternoon. Even though the inn was still under renovations, the girls had done a fantastic job creating an elegant, comfortable space for getting ready, even bringing in antique furniture from Penny's store.

The second Olivia caught sight of Eliza standing before the vintage mirror, her breath caught in her throat. She'd never seen a more magnificent wedding dress.

Delicate straps slipped over Eliza's shoulders with an uncanny resemblance to flowering vines, crisscrossing in a breathtaking pattern down her slender back. But the bottom of the gown truly stole the show. The silky white fabric of the skirt had been dipped in various shades of pink, creating a blossoming-flower effect as the ombre colors cascaded toward the hemline.

Tears sprang to Olivia's eyes as she took in the full breadth of Eliza's beauty. "You look exquisite," she breathed as Eliza turned to greet her.

"Thank you. I almost can't believe this day has finally come."

She gently caressed the white dahlia pinned in her hair, as if to make sure it was really there.

"It's all real. And you are the most beautiful bride. I can't wait to see Grant's expression when he catches his first glimpse of you." Olivia smiled wistfully, then added, "Cassie said you needed me for something?"

"Yes, I do." Eliza glided toward a rolling wardrobe rack where her veil waited to be worn. Sliding it aside, she grabbed a pale-blue dress.

Olivia frowned. She'd seen all the bridesmaids wearing their dresses already. Had one torn and needed repair?

"I need you to put this on," Eliza told her with a sly grin.

"I don't understand." Olivia glanced at her simple cocktail dress and comfortable high heels—her event coordinator uniform, as she called it, complete with understated hair and makeup.

"Liv," Eliza said gently, her gaze soft and warm. "Did you really think I could get married without you by my side? I didn't ask you sooner because I knew you'd use coordinating the wedding as an excuse. And when I asked Grant, he agreed that the slightly sneaky route would be our best option."

Stunned, Olivia gaped, struggling to sort through her emotions. She'd never been a bridesmaid before. And the touching gesture brought more tears to her eyes. But as moved as she was, she didn't see how it could possibly work. "I-I don't know what to say."

"You don't have to say anything," Eliza told her with a wide smile. "You just have to get dressed."

"But… someone *does* have to coordinate the ceremony," Olivia reminded her.

"Which is why Reed recommended the perfect person to stand in for you. Just for the ceremony, of course." Eliza nodded toward the back of the room, and Olivia followed her gaze.

At some point during the last few seconds, Isabella Russo had snuck into the room. She beamed at her. "I'll do my best to follow your schedule as seamlessly as possible."

"I— I'm speechless." Olivia couldn't move, too overcome with emotion, realizing everyone had banded together to make this happen.

"That's okay, you don't have to talk," Eliza reiterated with a playful wink. "But you *do* have to put on this dress."

"Are you ready for us?" Cassie asked, poking her head into the room.

"We sure are!" Eliza waved her in, and Cassie entered, followed by Lucy, Penny, Kat, and Sadie.

"We're your hair and makeup crew," Lucy announced, brandishing her makeup bag.

"Give me a few minutes before you do my mascara," Olivia said with a sniffle, fanning her tear-filled eyes.

Laughing warmly, the girls gathered around her, and someone turned on upbeat music as they set to work.

Olivia supposed that since she'd decided to stay in Poppy Creek, she'd have to get used to having a community who cared about her so completely. But truthfully, she didn't think she would ever get used to it.

For the rest of her life, she would count her blessings.

And in this town, she had a feeling that list would continually grow.

CHAPTER TWENTY-NINE

*A*s he stood in line with the other groomsmen, Reed's heart beat in a staccato rhythm, a sharp contrast to the dreamy, dulcet notes of "It Had to Be You" sublimely performed by a violin and cello duo.

He barely noticed Vinny trot down the aisle with his shaggy gray tail wagging as he proudly toted the ring satchel attached to his collar. Or Ben, clad in a dapper blue suit and bow tie, blowing playful, opalescent bubbles as he strolled down the petal-strewn walkway, an enormous grin on his face.

Reed's gaze remained fixed on the French doors, waiting for Olivia to emerge from the inn.

The second she stepped into the soft, golden-hour sunlight, a breathtaking vision in a sultry, strapless dress, his heart stopped beating.

While he'd never considered himself exceptionally eloquent, he couldn't imagine anyone being able to adequately encapsulate her beauty with words.

Warmth rippled through his body when she caught his eye and bestowed a tender, intimate smile that brightened her entire countenance. And he couldn't help wondering what it would be like to experience the moment all over again, but with Olivia as his bride.

At the thought, his vision blurred and he blinked rapidly, determined not to lose his composure.

But as she paused at the end of the aisle and gifted him with one last radiant smile, the emotion captured in her glistening eyes nearly pushed him over the edge.

He forced air in and out of his lungs, steadying his pulse as he stole a sidelong glance at the men standing beside him. They weren't any cooler or more collected than he was, each wearing similar enamored expressions as their better halves followed behind Olivia.

But as the music swelled in a crescendo, Eliza captivated everyone's attention as she floated toward them on her father's arm. Gasps and murmurs rustled through the throng of enthralled guests as she passed by, revealing the eye-catching and colorful details of her wedding dress.

While Eliza usually thrived in the spotlight, she barely seemed to notice the stir, completely transfixed by one person in particular.

Reed followed her gaze to Grant, who openly wept silent tears.

His own throat tightening, Reed recalled countless conversations with his childhood friend, appreciating how long he'd waited for this moment to arrive. The pair had endured more than their fair share of obstacles, but had faithfully persevered through them all, a testament to young and old alike.

After years of watching his friends settle down, Reed finally comprehended the unparalleled joy of finding his *person*, a partner in life who not only added to his happiness, but challenged, encouraged, and inspired him.

And, more clearly than ever, he understood the longing and conviction to say, *I do, until death do us part.*

Searching the crowd of enraptured faces, Reed caught sight

of his parents near the back row. His father's arm rested around his mother's shoulders in a simple, yet significant gesture.

A few weeks ago, he'd never imagined they'd get back together. But now, he couldn't fathom any other outcome.

Overcome with intense gratitude, he considered all the people in his life who'd been given a second chance—Grant and Eliza, his parents, and even himself.

He instinctively sought out Olivia, his heart melting when she met his gaze with a knowing glance, as though she'd had the same thoughts.

While he wouldn't recommend the road they'd walked, somehow, God had taken the dried, crushed petals of their lives and fashioned a new, vibrant bloom, more fragrant and beautiful than the one before.

And he intended to nurture and cherish the incomprehensible gift with each and every breath he had left.

*T*ears welled in Olivia's eyes as she watched Grant and Eliza whirl around the dance floor, performing each step of their choreographed dance with all the grace and flair of Fred Astaire and Ginger Rogers.

Their joy and delight diffused among the crowd of onlookers, illuminating the night more brightly than the thousands of twinkling bulbs glittering throughout the garden.

"I think you've set the bar for all the future weddings in Poppy Creek," Reed whispered in her ear, sending a pleasant shiver skittering up her spine.

"I hope that means you have confidence in your new business partner," she teased.

His dark eyes smoldered as he said, "Utmost confidence," and leaned in for a kiss.

But before their lips met, the DJ invited all couples to the dance floor to join the bride and groom.

"That means you, lovebirds," Lucy goaded with a playful grin.

Olivia flushed as the rest of their close-knit group joined Lucy's good-natured nudging, some a little more vocally than others.

At first, when they'd all found out about her and Reed, she'd been overwhelmed by their frenzy of mirth and excitement, not used to having so many people invested in her life and well-being.

Her brother had been the most overjoyed out of all of them. And the look on his face when he'd hugged Reed—visibly relieved, as though finally relinquishing the burden of worrying about her heart—had moved her to tears.

The other men had been less sentimental when voicing their approval. Colt had even started calling them *Reevia*, a combination of their two names that she wasn't wild about.

But despite some of the discomfort over the unexpected attention, she treasured being a part of a community, a group of men and women who genuinely cared about one another. And she couldn't be happier to finally call Poppy Creek her home.

"What do you say?" Reed held out his hand, a smile tilting the edge of his mouth.

When she slipped her hand into his, their overzealous friends hooted and hollered, deepening her blush.

"He said *all* the couples," Reed reminded them, attempting to disperse the unwanted audience.

With little resistance, everyone but Lucy and Sadie commingled on the dance floor, quickly lost in their own romantic bubbles.

Reed led her to a private corner and pulled her close, splaying his fingers against the silky bodice of her gown as he swayed to the music.

Heat from his palm penetrated the thin fabric, and her body

reacted with an involuntary tremor. Would she ever get used to the thrilling awareness? Or would it change and deepen over time as their intimacy grew? So much of what lay ahead remained unknown and uncharted. But rather than fear the future, she looked forward with hopeful anticipation, blissfully secure in the bond they shared.

"I can't believe I get to do life with you," Reed murmured, nestling his cheek against her curls. "Sometimes, I wake up and wonder if I dreamt it all."

Tilting her head back, she laced her fingers through his hair, stealing his breath with a kiss.

When she pulled away, a soft sigh escaped his lips and he kept his eyes closed a second longer, savoring every spine-tingling sensation.

"I figured, to show you it's real, I could either pinch you or kiss you," she teased.

"You made the right choice." He drew her closer, as though he couldn't get enough. "Although, with kisses like that, I don't know how we'll ever get any work done."

"You may have a point," she said with an impish smile. "But we'd better figure it out, because I've already booked our first event."

"You have?" He sounded pleased.

"Millie approached me earlier today about the Daisy Hop. Did you know this is the first year the town's had to skip the annual spring dance since its inception?"

"I didn't, but it sounds like the perfect inaugural event. When is it?"

"Next week." She laughed softly when his eyes widened in shock.

"Next week? Is that even possible?"

"Absolutely." She cupped his cheek, angling her lips toward his as she told him, "You just have to have a little faith."

EPILOGUE

*L*ucy Gardener absentmindedly prodded her colossal scoop of peanut butter cookie dough while she studied the dark figure across the crowded dance floor.

Aloof yet oddly alluring, Vick Johnson leaned against the thick trunk of the maple tree, shrouded in the shadows. In the dim lighting, she could barely make out the eagle tattoo on his forearm even though he'd rolled the sleeves of his charcoal gray button-down up to his elbows.

Normally, her fashion-forward sensibility would've balked at the bland color choice for a festive spring wedding, but she couldn't deny the way it accentuated his brooding gray eyes— eyes she couldn't get to notice her, no matter how hard she tried.

All evening, she'd received countless compliments on her appearance in the icy blue bridesmaid's dress. She'd even paid special attention to her makeup, expertly perfecting a naturally glamorous look. Which, incidentally, was considerably harder to achieve than a more obvious smoky eye or bold lipstick.

But no amount of effort made a difference. Vick remained resolutely impervious to her charm.

With a sigh, Lucy stuffed a spoonful of cookie dough into her mouth, risking her painstakingly applied lip liner. Not that it mattered, anyway.

Truthfully, she wasn't sure why she even cared. Once the inn opened, she'd move on to the next stage in her life—whatever that turned out to be—and put Poppy Creek, and Vick, in her rearview mirror.

Okay, so maybe she had a *tiny* inkling as to why his indifference bothered her so much. Completely unplanned, the stoic former marine had captured her interest when slim cracks in his hardened exterior provided a glimpse of his sweeter, softer side.

Lucy could usually read men far too easily. But Vick? She couldn't figure him out. Although, she desperately wanted to... more than she'd admit to herself, or anyone, for that matter.

Especially not her protective older brother, Jack, who happened to be his boss.

Well, *both* of their bosses, technically.

She tensed, already imagining the tirade Jack would unleash if he found out his precious little sister had a crush on the tattooed tough guy with a troubled past. It wasn't that Jack was judgmental, per se, but after Vick left the military, he'd floated from job to job without any apparent goals or direction.

Not to mention, he didn't stay in one town for more than a year or two.

At least that was one thing they had in common. Neither of them seemed to stay put for very long. Her parents called her flighty, but she preferred the term *free spirited*.

In the back of her mind, she intended to settle down one day. Except, she had no idea what she wanted to do with the rest of her life. And although she hid it well, her ever-growing anxiety swirled just beneath the surface nearly every waking second.

Whenever she broached her concerns with her mother, she heard the same empty assurance—with her beauty and charisma, she could have any successful man she wanted. Never mind that she *wanted* to be her own person with something to offer the world besides a pretty face.

"Hungry?" Sadie's teasing voice cut through her agitated thoughts.

Lucy glanced at her bowl, wincing when she realized she'd stress-binged the entire thing, down to the last chocolate sprinkle. "Great," she mumbled.

"Are you okay?" Sadie asked. "You were staring off into space pretty intently."

Blushing, Lucy stole a glance at the maple tree, relieved to find Vick had disappeared. "I'm fine. Just watching all the couples on the dance floor."

"I'm surprised you're not out there." Sadie gave her a playful nudge. "Look at all the eligible bachelors. I heard Grant's fancy-pants client Landon Morris is here."

Lucy smiled. Sadie must be worried about her since she never initiated typical girl talk, especially not gushing over handsome billionaires from Silicon Valley. "No, thanks. He's not my type."

"And who exactly *is* your type? You've been turning men away all night."

A popular line dancing song pulsed through the speakers, and Lucy grinned. "Why would I dance with a slick city boy when you're the best Boot Scootin' Boogier in town?" She set her bowl on a nearby table and grabbed Sadie's hand. "Let's show 'em how it's done."

Tugging her friend toward the dance floor, Lucy resolved to push Vick from her mind for the rest of the night.

And, if she could help it, a whole lot longer than that.

*K*eeping his head down to avoid eye contact, Vick Johnson slipped from the rollicking wedding reception into the quiet parking lot where cars covered every inch of gravel.

He strode toward his Jeep, pausing by the driver's side door to inhale a deep, cleansing breath.

Music and laughter wafted over the roof of the inn, but the crisp night air settled around his shoulders, offering a coveted sense of calm.

Re-centering himself after hours of exhausting chitchat and socializing, Vick gazed up at the vast expanse of ink-black sky overhead. He appreciated that no matter where he went in the world, the stars remained unchanged.

The social pressures and community-centric expectations of Grant and Eliza's wedding reminded him that it was almost time to move again.

Without realizing it, he'd become too comfortable here, too connected. In every other town, he'd been able to keep his distance. But the people of Poppy Creek had a way of drawing him into their fold whether he liked it or not.

And after everything he'd been through, he definitely didn't want to get attached.

Filling his lungs again, he tapped his fingertips against his thumb in practiced succession, utilizing the stress-relieving technique his last shrink at the VA hospital had taught him. While he wasn't convinced it helped, it didn't seem to hurt anything, either. And right now, he'd try just about anything to clear his head.

Especially after being distracted by Lucy Gardener all evening in that frustratingly flattering dress. He had zero doubt she knew exactly how good she looked, too, which irked him even more.

Over the last few months, ever since he volunteered to split his hours between flipping burgers at the diner and helping the construction crew at the inn, Vick found his attention drifting to his boss's kid sister more than he wanted to admit.

It wasn't that he *liked* Lucy or anything. At least, not in a romantic sense. He didn't date—period. Let alone someone so young and naïve. After a decade in the marines, he'd witnessed atrocities innocent little Lucy couldn't even fathom. And he wouldn't want her to imagine them, even if she could. He wouldn't wish the nightmares on anyone.

Tap, tap, tap....

He fidgeted with his fingertips again, still gazing at the stars.

Lucy grabbed his attention because she was beautiful and full of life, plain and simple. Like a colorful bird, a person couldn't help but notice whenever she fluttered by.

Fine, so she was sweet, too. And she could be funny, on occasion.

But it didn't matter.

Lucy Gardener was off-limits for more than one reason. More than a *hundred* reasons, if he really wanted to add them all up.

And the only way he'd get that into his thick skull would be to leave town as soon as possible.

He'd talk to Jack about it first thing in the morning.

Tonight, he'd go home, close his eyes, and stick a pin in his worn map of the United States.

He didn't care where he wound up.

But he couldn't stay here.

You can read more about Lucy and Vick, and catch up with your favorite Poppy Creek characters, in *The Whisper in Wind*.

Visit rachaelbloome.com and join the Secret Garden Club to receive exclusive bonus content and additional scenes.

AN UNLIKELY AUTHOR

First: A note about this blogpost.

I wrote it on March 28, 2019, several months before I'd published my first book. Why did I write it? Well, I explain that at the end. But all these years later, the words ring as true today as they did the first moment I jotted them down. And I hope they speak to your heart, too.

Without further ado…

It's no surprise Romance is the #1 selling genre.

We all crave love.

It's deeply rooted in who we are as human beings. Especially women.

Even as little girls, we dreamt about Once Upon a Time and Happily Ever After.

I know I did.

As a sweet romance author, most people assume I found my Happily Ever After at a young age. They imagine I married my childhood sweetheart and rode blissfully off into the sunset. I don't blame them. In some ways, it makes for a much better story. It's more "on brand."

But that sweet ideal couldn't be further from the truth.

I did marry at a young age. And at the time, I thought I'd found the kind of love I'd read about in romance novels—passionate, deep, everlasting love.

Then comes the part no one wants to read about.

Four years into our marriage, my husband told me he no longer loved me. In fact, he hadn't for a long time. I'll spare you the tears, the gut-wrenching pain, and the even less glamorous discovery that he'd written a new love story for himself with someone else. A heroine who, no doubt, had better hair, kept a cleaner kitchen, and who's bubbly, vivacious personality never faltered.

At twenty-five years old, I stopped believing in love. I scoffed at romantic comedies, rolled my eyes at sappy songs, and thought romance novels were a waste of paper. Something I should never, ever admit as a romance author!

For years afterward, I lived a life of shame and regret, trying to make relationships work, while harboring no hope they would.

One night after a recent breakup (and a tear-filled bath accompanied by every angst-ridden song on my iPhone), I made a decision. I couldn't live my life like this anymore.

The following Sunday, I went back to church. And on that sunny morning in early November, I met my husband, Philip, and my Second-Chance Romance began.

Now, before you say "Aww," I have to tell you something:

My Second-Chance Romance wasn't with my husband. It was with my Lord and Savior, Jesus Christ.

If you're still reading (and I hope you are), I want to share this truth with you:

You are loved. With a passionate, deep, and everlasting love.

Reconnecting with Jesus Christ healed my broken heart. He reminded me that my worth isn't based on one man's approval. I am not less than anyone else. I am not unlovable, undesirable, used-up, tossed aside, or unredeemable. I am saved by grace (Ephesians 2:8). A child of God (1 John 3:1). I am His masterpiece (Ephesians 2:10).

And so are you!

A few weeks after I met my husband, he asked me to dinner. To this day, he still teases me for turning him down.

But he graciously accepted that I wasn't ready. It took time for God to heal my wounds. And in some ways, He still is.

We remained friends, and six months later, he took me on our first date —go-cart racing, frozen yogurt, and a stroll by the river where we talked well past midnight.

Next month will mark two-and-a-half-years of marriage, and words can't describe how much I cherish and adore this man. Which is funny to admit as an author who's supposed to have all the words!

When I think about how far I've come—from denouncing love to penning romance novels—my heart fills with so much joy and gratitude I can hardly breathe.

I write because I enjoy it more than anything else. But I also feel compelled to write. Compelled to tell stories about women like me. Women who've felt broken, unworthy, and lost. And give these fictional women the gift of hope, redemption, and the love of an honorable man, which is only a tiny fragment—a mere glimpse—of the love God has for us.

While I might be the unlikeliest of romance authors, I hope my characters and stories resonate with you. And if anything I've shared speaks to you in any way, if you have deeper questions, or if you'd like to share your own thoughts and experiences on this topic, I'd love to hear them!

Your friend,

Rachael

ACKNOWLEDGMENTS

As always, this book wouldn't be in your hands today without the help of several talented professionals, many of whom are listed on the copyright page if you're looking to build your own dynamite team. Ana, Beth, Krista, and Trenda—you tirelessly whipped this book into shape, and I thank you.

Dave and Daria—your trusted insights mean the world to me, especially with a subject matter so close to my heart.

My Advanced Reader Team—you ladies are wonderful! I don't know what I'd do without you.

Special thanks, and all my love, to my friends and family who helped me grieve and grow through a difficult season. I'm so grateful you're in my life. Especially Philip, my most precious earthly gift and beautiful example of God's graciousness.

And lastly, thank YOU, dear reader, for joining me in Poppy Creek for five books and counting. If you enjoyed Olivia and

Reed's story, **please consider leaving an honest review at the retailer of your choice**. It truly helps new readers find the series.

Until next time...
    Blessings & Blooms,

Rachael Bloome

ABOUT THE AUTHOR

Rachael Bloome is a *hopeful* romantic. She loves every moment leading up to the first kiss, as well as each second after saying, "I do." Torn between her small-town roots and her passion for traveling the world, she weaves both into her stories- and her life!

Joyfully living in her very own love story, she enjoys spending time with her husband and two rescue dogs, Finley and Monkey. When she's not writing, helping to run the family coffee roasting business, or getting together with friends, she's busy planning their next big adventure!

COOKIE DOUGH BAR

May these recipes inspire fun, creativity, and lasting memories as much as they did for Olivia and our friends in Poppy Creek.

Classic Chocolate Chip

INGREDIENTS:

4 Tbs salted sweet cream butter, softened

1/4 cup light brown sugar

1/4 cup granulated sugar

1 tsp vanilla extract

2 Tbs cream (milk or milk substitute)

3/4 cup flour

1/4 cup semi-sweet chocolate chips

INSTRUCTIONS:

1. With mixer, beat butter on medium until smooth and creamy.

2. Add brown sugar and blend until smooth.

3. Add granulated sugar and blend until smooth.

4. Add vanilla extract and blend until combined.

5. Add cream and blend until combined.

6. Add flour 1/4 cup at a time, mixing in between until well combined.

7. Gently fold in chocolate chips.

8. Add additional toppings to taste.

Peanut Butter

INGREDIENTS:

3 Tbs salted sweet cream butter, softened

2 Tbs creamy peanut butter

1/4 cup light brown sugar

1/4 cup granulated sugar

1/2 tsp vanilla extract

2 Tbs cream (milk or milk substitute)

3/4 cup flour

INSTRUCTIONS:

1. With mixer, beat butter and peanut butter on medium until smooth and creamy.

2. Add brown sugar and blend until smooth.

3. Add granulated sugar and blend until smooth.

4. Add vanilla extract and blend until combined.

5. Add cream and blend until combined.

6. Add flour 1/4 cup at a time, mixing in between until well combined.

7. Add additional toppings to taste.

Tiramisu

INGREDIENTS:

4 Tbs salted sweet cream butter, softened

1/4 cup light brown sugar

1/4 cup granulated sugar

1/2 tsp vanilla extract

1 Tbs espresso (or strongly brewed coffee), cooled to room temperature

1 Tbs Kahlua (or more to taste)

3/4 cup flour

INSTRUCTIONS:

1. With mixer, beat butter on medium until smooth and creamy.

2. Add brown sugar and blend until smooth.

3. Add granulated sugar and blend until smooth.

4. Add vanilla extract and blend until combined.

5. Add espresso and Kahlua and blend until combined.

6. Add flour 1/4 cup at a time, mixing in between until well combined.

7. Add additional toppings to taste.

Additional Toppings

White chocolate chips

Crumbled brownie

Crushed chocolate covered espresso beans

Toffee bits

Sweetened coconut flakes

Toasted walnuts, pecans, or pralines

Chopped candy bars (Snickers, Butterfinger, Reese's, etc.)

Sprinkles

… or anything your heart desires!

Enjoy!

BOOK CLUB QUESTIONS

1. What are your thoughts regarding Olivia's predicament? How did you feel about her decision to keep the divorce a secret until after the wedding?

2. How did you feel about Harriet's transformation? Did her growth seem genuine?

3. What did you think about Reed's parents, Joan and Bruce, getting back together?

4. Out of all the people in Olivia's life lending words of wisdom, who do you think had the most impact (besides Reed)?

5. Is there anything in the story you wish had turned out differently?

6. What did you think of Harriet's metaphor about love, faith, and flowers? Do you agree or disagree?

7. Which of the characters did you relate to the most? And why?

8. What would you say is the overall theme of the novel? Was there more than one?

9. Were there any characters you'd like to read more about?

As always, I look forward to hearing your thoughts on the story. You can email your responses (or ask your own questions) at hello@rachaelbloome.com or post them in my private Facebook group, Rachael Bloome's Secret Garden Club, where I share sneak peeks and inspiration, ask for help deciding character names, and generally have an all-around great time!